Everything's Fuckin' Perfect
by
Barbara Helvey Hughes

Based Mostly on Truth

Forward and Dedication

Being Grateful and sane during the good times isn't difficult. When the shit hits the fan and the outlook is dire and you feel, think, know you have nowhere to go, no one to turn to who will understand and no faith left because it's all been drained out of you just by trying to keep it together - that's when you're most likely to have the opportunity to begin to understand that everything IS perfect.

Because when you see that glimmer of deep understanding within your thoughts, you know you are walking *through* the hellstorm and are no longer anchored inside it - forward movement is possible.

Keep putting one foot in front of the other. Keep moving ahead, with surety that even though you know there are many more storms ahead of you, you don't need to even think one small thought about them, because you're definitely on your way out of this one and you are growing.

It's during those times that we begin to see more clearly and can start to understand that everything is, *indeed*, perfect. We can start to believe it. Begin to see how it's bolstering everything else in our life.

None of us knows where our road will lead, how many forks we will face, how many obstacles or opportunities will clear or block our path, how many gauntlets we will be asked, or forced, to fight our way through…but, despite all of it (or maybe because of all of it) we persist. We prevail. We learn. We grow into the Soul we asked to be, before we ever arrived here. That's the beauty of it.

Anyway, I guess my point is that we never genuinely know from whence our Blessings may come – could be a Kindness of a Friend or a stranger. Blessings flow from many sources to each of us. Trying to connect the dots and reach a state of Gratitude is what we all yearn to stretch towards.

"Moving on" is very different from "moving forward". With 'moving on' we forget the 'why'. With 'moving forward', we remember the 'why', and also learn the lesson, insuring our inner growth.

The starting point for *Everything's Fuckin' Perfect (EFP)* was a lunch with one of my dearest Friends and one of Hughes Gallery's finest artists: Daniel. He'd been obsessing over something for two to three years and this particular day, I had suggested we have lunch at the, then, wonderful Boca Grande, FL restaurant The Loose Caboose, in the old railway depot on the island (Gasparilla), where Hughes Gallery, Inc. was located for almost a quarter of a century.

As we sat outside on their deck awaiting our grouper, I listened to Daniel drone on and on (sorry, Daniel) (we all do it) about topics we had discussed frequently (like every time we chatted), for what seemed like a millennium. I countered each and every comment with reasons why he should let this topic go and reminded him he'd already let it go and moved forward with his life. Or had he?

He wouldn't stop and I was impatient (my well-deserved middle name) and exasperated, because I Love Daniel and had been encouraging his emotional and Spiritual growth: just as he encourages mine.

Finally, after reminding him he had already dealt with these issues, and *somewhat* (but not completely) conscious that we were seated at an outside table in a standing room only area, but not really conscious of much of anything, except Daniel backpedaling at this particular moment...I looked at him, caught his eye and loudly blurted "Daniel, everything's fuckin' perfect - so why are you still rehashing this shit?!" His mouth slacked as he gazed around at every single person on the deck, some whom we knew, who were now glaring at me. He looked at me in disbelief and I, now fully aware of my gross faux pas, smiled weakly and tucked in for our lunch, which had just been served, bowed my head and awkwardly muttered 'sorry'.

I later thanked him for the conversation, because I realized that without that moment, I would, now, not have the title of this book. So, do I really have to say it...?

Everything's Fuckin' Perfect was conceived and written after the death of my husband, and brilliant artist, Jack R Hughes. You'll see him in the pages of this book...idyllicized, more often than not. So, Jack is for sure on my dedication list. Thanks, Jack.

Most importantly *EFP* is dedicated to my son, Chris, whose (whether he knows it or not) challenges have been my own, because most moms feel their kid's pain and discomfort,

4

joys and successes much more than anyone would ever suspect, especially their kids. Mirror.

Lastly, but certainly firstly in my heart and Soul, *Everything's Fuckin' Perfect* is dedicated with my deep Love and devotion to a guy I met, a couple of years after Jack's death, and who has walked with me, carried me through and sometimes even fanned the flames of my own hellstorms since Jack died: Peter McKinnon.

I've suspected since childhood that 'the God of my understanding' was not waiting for me around the corner with a baseball bat, ready to take me down at the height of my joy. Rather, my God just waits, just repeatedly attempts to present me with the lessons I requested to learn, before I accepted this organic shell of a house to live within, during this stretch of my Earth existence. Usually, those lessons and the connecting of dots on my end, can take years or even decades. My conversations with Peter often propelled me forward and generally forced me to rethink how I interpreted my life, my emotions, and the challenges I have faced and am currently facing.

I look back and realize Peter and I have been discussing all of those important things since we first met, and I can finally connect many of the dots within my particular matrix of a life. As much as I might have thought I needed Peter twenty or thirty years ago, the God of my understanding knew I first had to learn certain things, which would allow us to co-exist. I first had to face certain demons, first had to attempt to understand certain Universal Principles (my Larger Truths), first had to wallow, had to wait, had to Love despite feeling unloved.

I'm so Grateful I finally did learn some of those lessons, and I doubt they would have taken, without Jack and Chris in my life. I am Blessed beyond measure – and we can't really measure this stuff anyway….so, *Everything's Fuckin' Perfect.*

Thank you so very much for picking up and reading this book. You might love it, you might hate it, you might not finish it, but I hope you do, because I will promise you this: at some time in your amazing life, something written in these pages will barrel its way back to you and help you. That's a solemn promise.

With much Love and Brightest Blessings.
Barbara Helvey-Hughes
June 8, 2025

PREFACE

MARCH 14, 2016/PREFACE: This book is mostly true and based on the movie script I wrote back in 1994, *The Golden Thread,* which I posted on the American Zoetrope web site in '94 or '95.

A lot of what's happened through my entire life can be related back to recurring energies/spirits:

Niamh/Pathfinder/Jack
U'Niell/Declan
Murchad/Matt/NT

Some of the other shared life characters in this story are:

Biercheart/Eileen/LA
Dermot/Cain/JFC, Jr
Mahon/Raven's Moon/me

The above characters have had many, many more identities throughout their multiple and various lives, I'm sure, but these are the ones I've remembered, with regard to each of them and me, thus far.

These are the Three who have been with me for, well, forever. That is the storyline of the script and just about every dang thing I've written, for decades. Some things don't leave easy – they hook in and stay.

Maybe they haven't <u>all</u> been with me in every single life, maybe it's not always all three of them – maybe one, two, or three make it back with me; we decide one on one, before we ever arrive and then, it's a matter of the universe conspiring to throw us into the path of one another – or, not. Nothing's for sure. There are no mistakes (mis-takes), there are no accidents and, I believe, everything has intent and purpose so, whether we want to acknowledge, accept or believe it, or not – everything *is* fuckin' perfect!

I was alone. Well, we're never really alone, but I figured I was, way back then, you know, when I was a college sophomore and just starting my 'grown-up' path. I was searching – been a searcher all my life, this life. Not like Captain Sir Richard Francis Burton; no, no, more like Siddhartha.

Some inkling told me I'd better write this stuff down and that was, oh, about forty years ago and so, I did. Scraps of paper and half-filled notebooks and pages of scribbles and letters to myself and to others (unsent) and all kinds of writings all over my life, are stuffed here and there, filling boxes, cabinets, shelves, and bookcases. Notes and memories written out and wedged in books and used as bookmarks and written down as poems, short stories, movie scripts, plays, novelettes, etc., etc. I just simply could not

7

examine it all, in context and all at once, and complete, because it was too damn painful. I didn't have the heart: yeah, I have loads of heart, but a whole lot of it was expended on this particular time of my life and it was too much my Truth for me to look at it and write the entire thing down, to be read by others.

Angels have been scattered inside my life and around the perimeter, all my life, this time. I needed them, too. Back in college I was frantic about something, after Declan and before Richard and I was driving the MG just about as fast as she'd go, when I took that turn, you know the one coming out of Needmore, down from the old schoolhouse Weird Martha and I rented an apartment in, back in autumn, 1971. No, guess you don't know, so I'd better start the telling - here's the thing - something grabbed the steering wheel. Next thing I know, the car's sitting straddled across a ditch, and I've hit the steering wheel with my forehead and almost passed out. I swear I felt the fluttering of wings around me. I forced open the door. Fuckin'a, says I, lookin' around.

Now, this road wasn't your usual well-travelled highway…no, no, no….this was more like your Blue Highway, in fact, this might possibly be more like a well….purple or pink highway, meaning no one and I do mean NO ONE ever drove down this road, which was one of the many reasons I was so intent on renting that apartment in the old schoolhouse (but I guess at one time this road was like a super-highway back in the day, because of you know, the *schoolhouse*).

Yeah, when I returned to Bloomington and had missed registration, well, I just wanted to be out of circulation. Didn't want to see much of anyone and decided to get a job in the local RCA factory: might as well save some money for next semester or next year.

I gaze around the car and feel something. There's a familiar energy hovering about, but I can't, for the life of me, pinpoint it. In the weeds, back from the MG about 10 feet, were what looked like footprints – recent prints: just now prints. I stare at them.

They almost look like medieval boot prints, I think to myself. I don't know what that would look like, I think - no soles I guess. Wow, no souls, maybe: you know, the other soul. S-O-U-L. These are fresh - brand new.

Silent, I crouch down and touch one of the depressions: an energy races up my arm, which feels like something trying to electrocute me or pull me down into it. It's tearing at my heart. I stagger back. A frown runs across my forehead. Fear. Somewhere in the very distant back folds of my brain, a shade of a memory rises and floats forward. The memory is dark, dark. It's on the move and I don't want to allow it entry into my brain, in this current life. I rub my eyes and try to clear my thoughts, but it just keeps roaming forward. My heart races, I begin to sweat and feel as if someone/thing is stomping my heart – like there's a freakin' elephant's hoof resting on my chest and getting ready to make itself at home, despite my efforts to vanquish it. I fall back, into the weeds.

Maybe that should be the title of this damn book – *In the Weeds*.

What the heck was that and why was it possibly looking to harm me? I've lived a lot of lives – over the years, many 'readers' have told me I've lived many lives and well into my 90's and beyond, so I wasn't always too awfully terrible at warrioring, I guess. But I likely made some fierce enemies when I did wield the sword. I don't wanna remember.

This is, mostly, a true story. I can't just shine this stuff on. I have to tell it: because this is true and real and oh, so pure. Read on. Fill your heart. Cleanse your soul. Have Faith. Miracles happen all the time, we just have to recognize them, accept them, and embrace them. I should know - I've had an awful lot – a huge load of them. But, beyond that, when we each examine our lives, they are ALL Love stories and they are ALL miraculous, right until the very end.

We grow our way into our Love.

In most stories the reader falls in love with, or loves, certain characters. Maybe we wander into romantic love, fantasize and dream about a character; maybe we discover a character who lives the life we'd hoped to live; perhaps we love hating a singular character; we find someone we can beat up, so we don't beat up ourselves or others. Maybe we love certain qualities, the way a character thinks, expresses herself; or, the way a character moves the plot forward by his actions - maybe the way he allows the scenes to simply unfold and gather into, what becomes, his life.

I have loved all the characters who have found their way into all my lives – the ones planned, and those who didn't have a clue. Mostly I love the ones I've chosen over and over, and whether or not they return my love, in any given life, is irrelevant and inconsequential; because I understand they are all interwoven throughout all my lives, past, present and those to come. They are key players for me, as I am for them. There you have it: *Everything's Fuckin' Perfect.*

Anyhow, that's pretty much what's going on – I'm just relaying what I remember and hope you get a kick out of it.

10

Declan says it doesn't really matter to anyone, except me – I think he's wrong about that. I think we need Love stories. I think we need LOVE.

Be aware that this story shoots back and forth through time.

Oh, and BTW…that person tearing at my heart…. that person? It was…..me.

PREFACE ENDS

SAN FRANCISCO/APRIL 16, 1906: So, I'm at this hotel – yeah, check out this postcard – incredible, huh? New. How the hell did I get *here*? What year is it? Early twentieth century, for sure. California is 3,000 miles from Boca Grande, Florida. I don't recall actually *transporting* here – or, arriving here. This place is beyond gorgeous: but it's a city – no forests. I see why he's not here. I'm in California - alone! Where are they and how do I find them? My Three? Networks all down. We're on our own – ghosts shadow the machines and they ain't talkin'. Don't even know what the hell that means. OOPS. Am I thinking 2016? Help. Help me find them – you know they're key players & w/o them, I stop breathing, HartBreak. BHH ON A PALACE HOTEL POSTCARD, SF, CA/DATED1906

1918/COLORADO: I think it's 1918. In Colorado on an old Indian trail: Pathfinder would love this, but Pathfinder's dead and I don't know whether NT's alive or dead, himself. Mountains are new and angular – unlike the softer, ancient Blue Ridge. I'm heading for Eagle. Hard going, but I'm used to the hike. Thankful I have my bow and a few precious arrows. Bagged a rabbit late last eve. Hateful thing, this killing, but starving's even worse. Found a cave, built the fire low – just enough to cook the meat and stave off a chill. Getting to be near 'bout October, I'd guess. Aspens startin' to quake. Cold creepin' inta my bones & I need to think about getting to the valley. No map. No trail for NT and I'd swear he woulda come this way. He's Sioux, at heart. They're *all* Sioux. Wonder if he has the dogs (huskies) with him. Where the heck am I and how the heck do I get back to 2016 Boca Grande?! HeartBreak, Pathfinder…help. NT, help. All these lives. All these souls. How do I find them all? BHH/DIARY/DREAMWEAVING PAST LIVES DIARY/2025

1979/PARIS: Okay, okay…I'm on the Sacre Coeur steps and I'm feeling completely lost, even though I recognize where I am and know I've been here, before, but am uncertain what year this is. "What year is this?" I shout (in English). The French all glare at me. Holy cow, such *hostility* – and I love the French. Heck, Jack was a de Hewes before he became a Hughes. En quelle annee sommes-nous? Wow - I don't speak French. Studied Latin all those years, but not French. At least, I don't think I do. Attends une minute! Je pense en Francais! I scan the crowd, for NT or, someone. It would be just like the Universe to plop me down in Victorian France, as a woman, knowing I'm a 10th century Irish warrior. Reprogram! Someone hollers out – "mille neuf cent soixante-dix-neuf" …1979… How old am I? 28?! I look down at myself…I look at you. BHH/1979/GRAND TOUR

1979/MARRAKECH: OMG I might not find Declan or NT, but whatever year it is, Pathfinder, er, JACK is here. He, uh…He pulls out an Iranian passport. Persia? Karim? Didn't Persia save the world from stupidity or something, eons ago? He touches my face and worlds explode. Fractals everywhere. I travel through a band of light – a rainbow, I think. Snowflakes? Glitter globes?! Then, hot. Hot. Marrakech. Atlas Mountains. Sky of Stars. La Mamounia Hotel? Originally built by a king for his son in the 18th century and transformed into a hotel in 1923. Beautiful, but I stayed here in '79. Steal a glance in the humongous mirror: I'm wearing blue jeans and a t-shirt...okay....yeah, 1979; right, Karim? I'm confused! Look up – Karim (Jack) is still here. What's he doing here? I didn't know him, back then...he's talking to Declan Niall. What the...? Morocco/Declan – of course, I remember, now. NT approaches them and they all turn to me. Nightmare? My Three. LOST. Let's go, Karim – where's that magic carpet when you need it? Genie! BHH/1985/STUFFED INTO A PHOTO ALBUM FROM THE 1979 TRIP

1918/WESTERN TERRITORY/SPACESHIPS OVERHEAD: What year is it, now? 1918? S'mornin' opened my eyes and I'm starin' into the darkest eyes I ever seen. Probably Apache. Just sittin' cross-legged, starin' at me. Wow. Like a deer in headlights, I bolt up and jump back. He smiles. Stands. Reaches out a hand – I hesitate but take it. He leads me down to a most lovely stream – clear, swift running water. Looks deep. I dip my hand - not all that cold. He points to the hot springs, feeding it: nods. Walks away, givin' me some privacy. Although, I wouldn't mind his company - be careful what ya ask for, eh? Am still female. I strip and dive in, wash, swim back to shore only to find my clothes gone. Brain tanned buckskin pants and shirt in their place. I love the smell. Where the hell am I, and where the hell is everyone else? I thought I spotted a spaceship that morning, out on the horizon.
BHH/SCRIPT IDEA /1994/TILGHMAN ISLAND, MD

IRE/975AD: Back and forth, back and forth we spin, toward eternity. Forever unravels around us. Infinity can't stop laughing, but it's not joyful; rather, it's more akin to despair. We just planned our attack and I'm leading my best warriors along the River Nore. A dozen or so men slink into

13

water; they, hidden by the tall marshy reeds along the sides of the riverbank.

U' Neill hasn't a clue & he will wantonly slaughter me: my name is Mahon*. Ever the zealots, they will eventually hack down and destroy our clan's sacred tree: Maigh a' Daire*. Fire in the belly surges: consumes everything, everywhere. I look back at my most trusted warrior, Beircheart. Murchad. Dermot? He is with me – for now. Dair chants. The killing begins. Threads twist and knot and I feel the unseen hand ready to strike its blow. I turn. Dermot. Niamh…Love. Back and back, we curve.

I mount my stallion, Cahir. As his name translates, he is battle-worthy. We hasten toward the weeping fields.
U' Neill lags behind his men and sends one of his warriors roaring my way; his huge arm arcs upward, blade poised. The noise: deafening. Eagerly I ride forward, calculate the strike and reach my own mighty arm and sword outward. The clash leaves me reeling - pain shoots up my arm to my shoulder. Beircheart bellows, thrusts his blade deep into the throat of my attacker, grabs Cahir's reins. I slump as he leads us away. I rally - we slip off our mounts. I fall, wincing. Beircheart tears away my cloak and tunic. I gaze at the wound – what farce is this?! Inside me – what is it? Iron? I don't even know the concept of gear – but that's what that is! Befuddled, both of us. Some great spark, an arrow of fire, screams across the sky, as Beircheart and I stare, dumbfounded.
BHH/THE ORIGINAL STORY: *THE GOLDEN THREAD*/1994/FROM A DREAM JACK AND I SHARED.
*Mahon pronounced Mann – Brian Boru's older brother and one of the first southern kings of Thomond * Maigh a Daire –pronounced "moy ahr" sacred ancient oak of O'Mathghamhan (O'Mahony) & O'Brian clans*

1970/BLOMINGTON, IN: Far off, in the far, far distance I spot Dermot – JFC, Jr., I knew he was a contentious bugger. Pathfinder morphs to Jack/Niamh(!).
Murchad/Matt becomes NT; finally. You're here. Beircheart becomes Eileen/Cahir/LA. As U' Neill approaches, his cloak and 10th century clothing falls away, revealing blue jeans & a dark pageboy haircut. His green eyes spark: he smiles from ear to ear – wow, I know that face – I'm gazing at Declan Niall. I'm now a woman, and happy to be one at this particular moment. I reach for…..Wait! I can't ….I won't….my head thrown back: it almost feels as if my neck will snap…I'm in the vortex so fast, my thought processes lag behind my physical body a couple of seconds and it takes a bit to figure out I'm jumping toward another time/place.
BHH/THIS INFO DISCOVERED IN THE MARGINS OF A PAPERBACK EDITION OF THE HOBBIT, AND NEXT TO THE POEM, *THE ROAD GOES EVER ON AND ON* by J.R.R. TOLKIEN, OWNED AND DATED (1961) BY TEN-YEAR OLD BARBARA A. HELVEY

2016/GASPARILLA ISLAND BRIDGE: Driving across this morning, the water flashed that gorgeous blue/green color I love so much. Looking closer, I noticed a peculiarity – it looked as though raindrops were bombarding the small sections of each wavelet. The tide was in and it wasn't raining. What's going on?! No wind, no rain - nothing, except those small bullet type holes drilling down into the water. What the heck causes that, I wonder?!
Awwww….why'd ya have to ask, Brain? NOOOOO! I have dinner to fix tomorrow, for a friend's birthday, PUT ME BACK! BHH/SCRIBBLED ON THE BACK OF AN ELECTRIC BILL ENVELOPE

1958/GREAT LAKES/LAKE MICHIGAN: and I'm alone, standing on a dune, facing Lake Michigan. My Grandpa's cottage sits a short distance away. A dark, brooding storm brews off in the West. I can barely see the top of the cloud it reaches so high. No bird calls. No sounds at all. No wind. Nothing, except fear, stalking toward me...storm coming on like a mountain scraping at the sky, trying to lick away the clouds; but the clouds barrel on, toward shore (and, me): dark, ominous clouds. Suddenly, the approaching aggregate sounds like a monstrous freight train, speeding up, readying to mow me down. Intent, the wind darn-near lifts me away, but I anchor myself, digging into the sand, head down; eyes covered. Sand pounds my backside, like needles or ten thousand darts...then, quiet. It's gone. I wait a sec, stand.

I'm seven years old and there's a boy, about eight, silently watching me. Eyes bore right into my soul. I shudder. I didn't see him, at first. He blended. Now, there he is. Here I am. I know him. I will meet him in college. I know I will. He has the most beautiful green eyes I've ever seen. My own eyes are grey shot with gold, and they are keenly watching him, watch me. He silently approaches, takes my hand. I'm Declan, says he. I'm Barbara, says I. We struggle to the top of the dune and slide down, gleeful.

At the bottom, another boy, about twelve, laughs; his body stretched out in the pillowed sand, and he, looking, smiling at the clouds. Whaddya think that one is? Oh! I know, I know – look at that, there's a deer and an Injun, waiting to get it with his bow, says he. He glows at me. I'm Jack - you like ta fish? I nod. Declan glares at Jack. I smile – I recognize him and look from him back to Declan and back to Jack. Jack's smile quickly fades when he realizes the hate in Declan's eyes is for him. Jack rises and skedaddles. Whadja go an' scare him away? Declan shrugs. You're mine

this time. Don't be so sure, says I. You ain't King of the Hill, yet, Declan, and don't you forget it. Pain snaps in his eyes and he slowly disintegrates, fades and, finally, disappears. I stand, alone, and cry. I *weep*. Why are these chains around me so tight?
BHH/DIARY/1972 FROM MEMORY & STILL WEEPING

1860/IRE/CORK: Nine-year-old Eileen calls to the tribe and seemingly, from nowhere, at least a dozen nine-, ten- and eleven-year-olds materialize out from behind trees, bushes, sheds - everywhere. She glowers at them, casting her long gaze on each, one by one, roasting them and daring them to jump off that grill. It's over, says she, Clare's King of the Hill. Clare can't BE King of the hill, says Dermot, his hazel eyes flashing: she's a girl. Can't be King if you're a 'she'. God, he's just so stupid, says Eileen, under her breath. That's how much you know, yells Eileen, angered even more. They all shrink, except Dermot, who glowers right back. Clare sees the exchange and heads for Eileen….stop, says she – right now, just stop, Eileen, k? Eileen leans to Clare. You gonna make me let *him* win, Clare? Clare skips over to Dermot, smiles, and takes his hand. C'mon, don't be mad, jus' 'cause I won King a' the Hill, Dermot…k? That anger hurts your soul, Joe…er, Dermot.
BHH/JOTTED IN 1960 by BARB HELVEY, ON THE END PAGES OF A TRIXIE BELDEN BOOK, *THE GATEHOUSE MYSTERY,* by JULIE CAMPBELL TATHAM ©1951 – IDEA FOR STORY: *PATTERNS*. DAMN, HAS IT BEEN ONE HUNDRED YEARS ALREADY?!

1972, FT. LAUDERDALE, FL/ SPRING BREAK: Your long-ago name was Cain? says I. He shakes his head yes. I know you, from Bloomington, don't I? Another yes nod. Can't believe you don't remember me, Barb, says he. Oh, I

do, I do - all that trying to forget didn't help one bit.
Wow…careful, Girl. This one's dangerous. He smirks.

Hey, didn't your mom make you marry some local girl, says
I? The one you told me you didn't want to marry?

He snarls. I lean in. Didn't work, before, says I, why would
you think it would work, now, Joe? I know you know and it
may not play out the way you thought it would/should, but
everything is perfectly perfect, Joe. You shouldn't have gone
to Viet Nam.
BHH/ON A SCRAP PIECE OF PAPER STUFFED
INTO OMAR KHAYYAM'S *THE RUBAIYAT*/1872/
THIRD EDITION/TRANSLATED BY EDWARD
FITZGERALD/OWNED BY BARBARA HELVEY
HUGHES. 1988

Everything's Fuckin' Perfect
(First Turning Point)
By
Barbara A. Helvey Hughes

May 30, 1971, and most of my college friends had already
left for home: summer jobs, vacations, study elsewhere. It
was my twentieth birthday, and I was drowning in a sense of
urgency I used to feel, when I was younger and alone.
Hormones? Emotions? Loneliness? Don't know, don't care
what the label would be – I was in the middle of it and
needed relief; someone to share my birthday with, someone
to let me know all was well. Thank God, you weren't
around back then, Jack. You would have left me in tatters. I
ended up fairly shredded as it was.

But this story really begins several months prior to my
twentieth. In August 1969, I entered Indiana University as a

18

freshman. Bloomington was two or three times larger than my hometown and I loved it: meeting people from all over the world - people who exposed my mind to wondrous ideas - people for whom everything was possible and there existed no barriers, no limits, no confines. It was an exciting time, a scary time, and a time of genuine opportunities to change whatever we disliked about ourselves and about the general world around us. Fuckin'a and far out!

I felt his eyes. Felt his energy and it wasn't threatening – it was uneasy, like he wanted to say something, but just couldn't come up to me and start talking. There was something contemplative about him, regarding me: but not so much in what I eventually saw of his regular life. In his normal day-to-day existence, he could be cavalier and impulsive. He was a Gemini (flip my hair, 'so what's your sign?') Me, too. Trouble. Capital T.

He was one of my Three. Number One in fact. I knew it from the start and I knew our paths must intersect and that he was the One. My One. The One I must find. Yes, and he was the first. We'd shared many lives together and I knew it, immediately: some pivotal ones. Would I lose him? How I loved him, from the moment I first saw him – from the time I was seven years old - but I'm getting ahead of myself, and I need to do this in order. I need to remember this, correctly, because I've said I'll write it out for so many years and haven't. It's begging now. I have the time now. And so, it begins. There he is. Here I am.

The Student Union was where I usually ended up between classes. Easy for me to focus and tune out distractions, especially when it was something I was genuinely interested in - which was just about everything I studied at IU. I remember sitting, facing the bowling alley, knowing someone was watching. A couple times over the weeks and months when this was happening, I stood and moved around the tables, scoping out who was there and seeing if I knew anyone. I always did, but never the one who was watching. His eyes bored through me, and yet, I could never pinpoint them. He was evasive. Not in a negative way, just in an "I'm watching and waiting, and I'll meet you when the time is right" way. You know – Moody Blues, *Watching and Waiting* kinda thing.

In the meanwhile, someone else kept placing notes under the wiper blade on my MG midget. I'd come out of the health food store and there would be a note, in all caps: "I'M WATCHING YOU". Really?! I just shook my head and leaned against the car, turned my head around and finally shot my middle finger up, so whoever it was would be sure to see the gesture. This one really bugged me, because he was much more overt and devious. I felt the energy and knew this guy would reveal himself – probably sooner than the other one. This one pissed me off something terrible. Yeah, Joe/Cain/Dermot. He was manipulative. I intuitively knew he would cause enormous trouble in my life. Unrest. There would be no peace if he was allowed access to my life and to my emotions. I also knew he was not one of my Three. He had traveled with me, many times, but often on contentious terms. This was the beginning of my path toward awareness. Nothing like a bit of combativeness to wake us up.

It was a freakin' freezing day; clear, crisp, and gorgeous with a sky so blue it almost me made me weep. Fat, billowy clouds ran across the blue, behind sharp, bare limbs of trees, naked for winter. Brrr. Colder than yippy fuck.

20

Don't know where that saying came from, but we all said it to describe, well, mostly the cold, back then.

It was probably November or December 1970 when I raced down the five or six wide banks of steps, leading out of the Student Union and spotted Amanda (Mandy) Rainwater, running toward the building; we stopped and hugged. We were both on our way to classes – she toward Ballantine Hall and I, way across campus, to the business building. We were getting ready to say goodbye when I **felt** someone approach. Amanda said "Oh, hi, Dec." Suddenly a tall 20-something guy, with very dark shoulder length hair and green eyes stood in front of me, his eyes locked on mine. He had one heck of an intense stare. I know, I know – sounds so corny when I write it, but it's true. His gaze was like a tracking beam of an alien ship, and I was captured. After what seemed like a lifetime and Amanda introducing us (Barb, this is Declan Niall; Dec this is Barb Helvey) we still couldn't unlock, and Amanda finally said "Hey! What's going on? Do you guys know each other? Man, you oughta start your own electric company!" I swear that's what she said. She must have felt the immense energy jumping between us, which almost took me down.

I smiled, I think; said something banal, like 'nice to meet you' and practically ran away. I did look back. He stood there, staring at me. Wish I'd had hyper-drive back then. But I didn't and I was wearing knee high boots with slick heels and a rust-colored wrap around wool maxi-coat: walk-running and trying not to slip and fall. Had on L'Heure Bleue perfume and it kept wafting around me: shit, I almost fainted. Funny how we can remember so many details about stuff that happened many years ago and can't

21

remember what we had for supper, last night. Guess I'd better get used to it.

After that I didn't see him again, except for a glimpse here and there, and he was always with a woman. She was tall, like him. She looked older than me – I was nineteen. One evening, probably in mid-April 1971, some friends asked me to go with them to see our mutual friend, Jimbo, who lived with a bunch of other guys in an off-campus house on the edge of town. My friend, Red, rode with me. I climbed three very steep, long stretches of steps and stood on the porch, looking down to the street. I **felt** someone behind me and turned. Declan stood in the doorway, behind the screen door, quiet and smiling. He opened the door – it creaked. "You comin' in?" Yeah, I was - and I did....

Walked into the living room, where Jimbo was passing around the biggest joint I'd ever seen. It looked like a huge cigar. I took a hit (yeah, I *inhaled*) and passed it on. Declan was holding up the archway: leaning into it with his arms crossed, looking at me, smiling. God, he had the most beautiful smile. I can still see him. I hugged Jimbo and whispered, 'Where's the kitchen?' he pointed. Dec was no longer in the arch, and I hurried out to find something to get rid of the dryness that had suddenly invaded my mouth.

In the kitchen I startled to find him at the sink, filling a glass with water. He held it out and smiled. I stood there like an idiot, mute and staring. Suddenly another energy entered the room and said, 'My name's Abby and I live with Dec. (a beat) Better take that water.' I turned and, towering over me, was the Amazon woman I'd seen him with every time I saw him over the past few months.

22

I said nothing and stalked toward the front screen door. Red hollered from the living room, 'Hey, Barb, I'll catch a ride'. I nodded and started away. I heard Declan's footfall behind me and I picked up speed. As I got to the door, he caught up and spun me around. He handed me the water, after he took a sip. 'Take the water.' I did. I gulped it down, without a word and scowled at him. All he said was 'When it's right, I'll see you again, but I'm leaving town for a while.' I looked behind Declan, into the house. Abby was coming at us, fast.

I leaned into him and said 'I don't play games', then I escaped. I had no idea what all this meant, but I did know I was completely in love with a man I knew absolutely nothing about. I mean, as in love as a nineteen-year-old hippie chick could be, right? But I didn't know where he was from, didn't know his age, if he was in school, in love with Abby (must not be). I based everything I felt on the intermingling of our energies. And the fact that I knew he was the one watching me, and I loved his energy; well, mostly anyhow, from the Lake Michigan incident. Glad to see him return to me. I knew I was supposed to be with him, in some capacity, but I was still a virgin and didn't really have a clue - to say I was naive is, well, yeah, quite the understatement.

Abruptly, I stopped seeing him. He simply disappeared. Almost two months passed and I looked everywhere I thought he might hang out. Even Mandy hadn't seen him, and they were friends. Seems he did play those games, but I didn't understand the rules. So, here we go again.....

May 30, 1971, and most of my college friends had already left for home: summer jobs, vacations, study elsewhere. It

23

was my twentieth birthday, and I was drowning in a sense of urgency I used to feel, when I was younger and alone. Hormones? Emotions? Loneliness? Don't know, don't care what the label would be – I was in the middle of it and needed relief; someone to share my birthday with, someone to let me know all was well. Had the MG's top down and was racing along one of the streets, which would lead me out of town and into the beautiful countryside surrounding Bloomington. I think I might have stopped by to see my friend, Clyde, on my way out of town. I was restless and alone – not a good combo for me, back then.

Shifted into 3rd gear and the engine whined wanting to go faster and into 4th, as I passed the Tao Bakery: Declan spotted me, shot his thumb in the air and plastered a huge smile across his face, as I skidded to a stop. Like he *knew* I'd be passing. He dumped his backpack behind the seats and neither of us could stop staring at the other. He leaped into the seat. Heat. Heat. Heat.

Where to? says I. Needmore, says he and off we went to the infamous hippie nudist colony.

It was late early afternoon as we cruised to one of the lakes and stopped. He spotted a canoe and helped me into it, lit a joint and passed it to me. We must've looked pretty goofy just staring at each other with stoned out smiles plastered on our faces. While he rowed, we talked, a bit. He was a year older and his birthday was coming up – a Gemini, just like me! He'd been in California and returned a couple days before and was living in a cottage not far from the lake. The energy popped and crackled between us, as it had during our first meeting. I recall a kind of serenity, because we'd reconnected. I hadn't been sure I'd ever see him again.

24

Now, forty-six years later and hundreds of Google searches later and I can't find him, again – like he disappeared into thin air. No obit, no trace - weird. Where R U Declan Niall??? BHH/GOOGLING

1976/DATE UNSURE/EASTERN AIRLINES: Flying to NYC and there's a girl, sitting next to me, who has a striking resemblance (in my mind) to Haley Mills. We strike up a conversation. She suggests I try a Bloody Mary made with rum, rather than vodka - what the hell - I'm up for most anything. I did. Boy, that's yummy and it becomes my preferred drink. Sweet, like me? Uh, no doubt.

So, we begin talking and I tell her I went to college at I.U. in Bloomington. She used to live there. I ask her (as I ask *everyone*) Do you know Declan Niall? She sucks in her breath. Wow, says she, are you, *Barbara*??? You are! I know you are!

I'm a bit embarrassed and ask Where is he? Have no idea, he was heading to…somewhere, can't remember last I even saw him. Well, says I, where are you headin', now? Not where he'd be, Barbara…Can you tell him I'm looking for him? says I. I hand over my address and phone. Sure, says she. I'll do that, if I see him.

I never heard a word from either of them, ever again.

Don't you *get it*?! If one teeny, tiny thing hadn't happened the way it did, we would not have met.

BHH/IN AN OLD ADDRESS BOOK, ON A SCRAP PIECE OF PAPER /DATED 1982/COVERED WITH QUESTION MARKS: A mere 30 miles separated us all those years when we were growing up. Wow, thirty freakin' miles: coulda been ten thousand.

2009/INDIANA/GOIN' HOME: All the times I've driven past the road, which leads to Kokomo, Indiana and I've never had the guts to go ahead and drive to the high school and see if Declan actually went there. I have to wonder why.

Mom just passed away in my arms and I can't even think. Declan is the very last person on my mind; well, that's a bold face lie and I know it. Damn. Truth hurts and I'm bleeding out, here. C'mon, fast forward.
BHH/2010 DIARY *AFTER MOM, NUMBER THREE*

2016/HUGHES GALLERY/BOCA GRANDE, FL: Sitting at my computer and thinking about all these connections. I seem to be making them daily, now. Here we go, again – it's a wild ride:

Last autumn, I met an important soul from one of my past lives; possibly more than one. Let's call him NT. His energy was so familiar that I recognized it immediately. Meeting him shook me up - so much so that I told a dear friend about him and I don't normally share this past life information with very many people. She asked the usual questions: his name, what he looks like, where he lives etc. I had no idea and couldn't answer most of them; but I told her his energy is blue and yellow, just like mine and I saw it every time I thought of him.

He said he would email me to find out if I'd gone on a trip, after the unexpected and recent death of my husband of thirty-three years (Jack). I was thinking about visiting our son and his family. Didn't want to be alone that first Christmas. Yes, I went. Yes, he emailed.

There's a definite connection – a soulful connection. At our first meeting, in this life, he asked if he could hug me. I understood, since I often empathetically hug people, whom I've just met. It's a compulsion, for a giver, to comfort one who hurts. I was hurting. I hesitated, because I'd known him, and known him well, in the other life.

I doubt he recognized me and although I know he has a bright spiritual element, I wonder if any of these specific concepts are even a part of his spiritual, emotional, intellectual makeup this time around.

We all seem to ignite the flames of who we each are, according to what we each need in every individual life we live – these perceptions might not even be on his radar.

NT became a kind of muse and inspired me to write wonderful stuff, personal stuff and it seems I've hit a stride, stimulated by him, where my expressiveness peaks higher and higher.

I cannot un-know him – he is a large part of my eternal journey and to connect with him, again, on any level seems almost too fortuitous at this particular juncture on my spiritual path. Since becoming 'Barbara', only three of these deep-rooted partners have been revealed to me – he is the third. My sacred number is three. Does that mean anything?

I've found and recognized many, many souls from past lives – many spirits, whom I profoundly love; but only three with whom I've traveled these more difficult paths and, without whom, I admit to feeling a bit lost. Even as a male in other lives, these three have had my back in order for me to live my intentions and accomplish my goals. We were warriors. We were wives, husbands, teachers, monks, champions, mentors, brothers, counselors, sisters, and all things. These are important souls in my vast circle.

He's walked through his fair share of fear: he's been in many dangerous situations during his life. But this stuff is the genuinely scary stuff, for most of us. This is heart-stuff, emotion-stuff, spirit-stuff, and we can talk all we want about possibilities and opportunities; but when one jumps in our faces in the middle of our road, more than halfway through our lives and which won't be ignored – that's different.

Nothing like fear to chain us to our supposed realities. Nothing like fear to keep us in line. Nothing like fear…except Spirit. But that's another chapter. Peace. Peace? Yeah, I get it.

I had awakened from a dream and emailed him. Knowing he'd been awakened at the same exact moment did not frighten me. Jack and I jumped into each other's dreams all the time. You know…I'm fearless. I know he's fearless, too.

I do not believe in chance. So what lesson am I to internalize? What will I allow to travel with me? Will he, eventually, take any of this to heart – into his heart? I think he has already. I think he's already thinking – how could I so dearly love one, who did not? I could not.

Because I also believe everything in our lives is absolutely perfect, I must believe we were meant to meet again and in these specific, exact circumstances. He found me. Period. That was the imperative. We cannot un-meet.

28

I can't read the minds of others – even those I love. I cannot predict the now, or the future. I have little, in this respect, to recommend me and I have much less if I allow myself to dwell upon it. But I must dwell upon it.

I don't believe I can ever find another Jack – or, that I should or that I need to – that isn't the point of the reintroduction of NT to me in this particular life. Jack and I shared an integral link and an irreplaceable synergy, which almost supersedes - no, which <u>does</u> supersede this earthly realm: this time, this place. Jack and I are halves of a whole – we are each other's hyperlink to the universe and it's a significant link stretching back to the beginning. I don't doubt Jack was Barbara and Barbara was Jack. I won't even attempt to explain these statements, except to say Jack would get it and I'd never have to even attempt to explain it to him. Jack once told me, this time, he waited a thousand years for me.

So, NT isn't a "Jack replacement", rather, he is another intrinsic part of me and I of him. We are also bound in an eternal embrace. But, why now? Why would we meet, *now*? I cannot answer these questions and believe they don't need answering. Some things simply are. And, anyhow, I *know* why. We would not be the souls, energies we are, without one another in some capacity in this life, as well as in the other(s). How we add to, and assist, one another is truly a thing of beauty. I'm so grateful I'm able to connect some of these dots.

They are important. They are immensely beautiful.

Love.

Wow.

Sometimes, I feel as if I'm gathering stars.

Sometimes, stones…

BHH/LOST? AFTER JACK LEFT/2016/WRITTEN
FOR NT's BIRTHDAY

MARCH 6, 2016/BOCA GRANDE – THE OTHER
'BOCA': Boy, life is so strange, wonderful, exciting,
mundane, interesting - how many adjectives do we really
have time for at this point in our lives, with more than half
of our lives gone and who knows how much left?

Last night I hosted a birthday party – couldn't have invited
a finer group of humans to my house and cooked dinner for
them…they are all stellar. STARS, Darlin'. I AM gathering
stars and I love it when that happens. I GET it.

(Jack, you see that silver disc last night? Same one as used
to hover about the cabin three summers ago: 2016 - PS
There's a stone in my heart, where a star should be.)

BHH/BG/ MAYBE NOBOBY GETS IT AND WE'RE
ALL JUST WANDERING AROUND OUT
HERE/SCRIBBLED ON THE DVD SLEEVE FIRST
SEASON *LOST*

2016/NORTH CAROLINA/BLUE RIDGE
CABIN/RAVENSWOOD – 7am:
        Namaste, Dear One. First, thank you for bringing
me into your circle of trust. Maybe the only way to
genuinely get to know a fellow human traveler is to take a
leap of Love and, therefore, faith and trust , and open
ourselves up by sharing the very experiences we find most

difficult to share with others. Nothing is sincerely easy when we make the decision to trust another enough to share painful or intimate details about our lives – things we don't *have* to share but make the conscious decision to do so.

Our veneers are often only skin deep. It's when we attempt to burrow down deeper that we hit the chains and locks bound around our hearts and spirits: our truest 'selves'.

I often think about when we built my studio, a couple years ago. I grabbed a spade and went digging, out in the front of it. I'd done as Jack suggested and graphed out a diagram - where I wanted gravel pathways and groupings of my favourite flowers for bouquets. Back in Maryland, I had hundred-year-old rose bushes and Jack had bought me a lilac bush for Mother's Day, hydrangeas (blue and gorgeous – he had such a green thumb) and the peonies were heavenly – plump and full and flamboyant. He'd planted my very favourite daisies and lilies and all kinds of flowers. It was a riot of colour. Down the road from the island, was a gladiola farm – another of my favourites. But in front of my NC studio, I'd hope to plant a wide variety of flowers and herbs. High on the list were dahlias and zinnias. Jack's Aunt B in Tennessee saved me seeds from plants, which dated back to her own Mother's time. I was jazzed!

And, eager to get digging - by my very genetic nature, I'm not real gentle – I have to think about it. C'mon…I'm more warrior than monk. When I was in college, 1970, my then boyfriend, (yes, I did date him.) JFC, Jr. used to tell me he always knew when I was approaching – I have a hard, firm step – aggressive, almost and I'd always wore Frye shit-kicker boots, because I loved to ride in the mornings. It's just that warrior gene – who am I kidding?

31

And so, I attacked the earth with my trusty spade, and I do mean attacked: assault on all fronts - digging, digging, digging. I went at it with all the force and gusto I could muster and then, unexpectedly, I hit solid rock and a shock, like a painful, electric current, shot up my arms and into my shoulders and back and I had to almost bite my tongue not to holler at the top of my lungs! I had no idea our beautiful dirt was a mere twelve inches deep in most places.

Why am I telling you this? I already know you have patience with me and I Love you for that. I am, firstly, a writer and lover of words and syntax. Hopefully, this will not bore you. Generally, I eventually get to the point albeit usually by some circuitous route. Many people are sort of like that plot of land, up there, in front of my studio. Dig down a few inches, even attempt to make some headway into discovering who they really are and we hit what seems like stainless steel doors - eventually, even the strongest, most valiant of us will turn and walk away.

Trying to get to know another can be a daunting task. Many won't even attempt to dive deep and they, consequently, travel only on and around the surface of those so-called friendships. I'm not like that and I sense you aren't either – I know you're not, because I know you. That statement in, and of, itself can and would be frightening to many. You have not questioned me (not overtly, at least) when I say those things. I don't know if it's because you think I'm circling the inner rim of insanity (think Ryans – on both sides) or because you're such a gentleman that you would never confront me about these statements (I know you are that), or, because you do, truly, understand it when I say that and you do, truly, Love me on a certain level. I think it's the latter.
I hope, at least.

32

It's always been easy for me to love – it's in my nature; but as you get to know me, on a deeper, fuller level, you might begin to think I can be fairly guarded/reserved. (Not with you, because of so many factors, but with others.) It's the impenetrable level we hit when things get 'real'. (When Cameron was a little boy, did you ever read him *The Velveteen Rabbit?* It's a sweet story about a group of toys and a stuffed rabbit struggling toward the goal of learning to become *real.*)

You know what I mean – when things get to a certain point, each of us has the opportunity to proceed with/in Love or to pull back a bit and 'regroup'. I've come to understand for me, when I retreat, it's simply my ego in action. I'm not wanting to put myself, my life, my experiences, my family, thoughts, insecurities, ideas, conflicts, problems/challenges etc., etc. out there for others to <u>try</u> to process, and heaven forbid, to judge – it all goes back to control. Or, more accurately, lack of it. All any of us really want is to be Loved and to Love: it's the difference between Love and love, where the courage appears (or, doesn't).

I awakened this morning thinking of you and your family – and courage. In my mind, things like courage directly link to Love. I guess all of the empathetic, compassionate, and positive emotions must (by their very nature) tether, consciously, back to their origins in Love. Love can't birth a negative emotion – it would be completely impossible for that to happen.

Okay, so now you get that all of the above was the set up for the *real* stuff:
For the past several years, I've been writing *Notes from Mom* and *Everything's Fuckin' Perfect.*

33

I do hope my (occasional) crudeness does not offend your sensibilities – as a Southern Gentleman, I know it can be difficult to hear a woman, possibly at times, even a *Lady* use these sorts of sailor-esque kinds of words, but as Evelyn so famously said, after ramming into the two girl's VW, after they zipped into the parking space she was awaiting: "TOWANDA!" TOWANDA must be a Secret Southern Cuss Word (SSCW). Seems to me to be a pretty damned great comeback for most offenses – or, as Barbara Helvey Hughes has said, "fuck 'em if they can't take a joke." Not meaning *you*, in particular, but just folks, in general. The "f" word just doesn't carry the punch it did, when no one said it! You know?

I remember sitting on our front porch, watching, and waiting as a wall of beautiful fog arose from the valley and began its slow, decisive trek up the mountain ranges, in front of the cabin. I was writing about courage when this happened. Jack was rooting more deeply into not only physical challenges, but also mental ones (that's another story). Standing outside, looking in as I was (since I couldn't jump into his skin, like I'd wanted, in order to better understand where he was and what his thought processes were) I realized just how amazingly courageous my darling Jack had been, and for many years. We simply cannot know nor can we completely understand what someone else walks through. We try our best to empathize and engage with compassion, but some things are meant to be singularly experienced, I guess.

The fog, slowly, approached the cabin – it was so lovely, it made my heart flutter. It seemed almost human. Gosh, I looked and looked this morning for that diary and can't find it, so I'm winging it, here. As I sat there, waiting to surrender to, or escape from, the inevitable fog, I began writing the chapter on courage. I should give you a wee bit

34

of background on this book, I guess. These things don't just happen in a vacuum – nothing does, does it?

Eleven months after our grandson was born, our son appeared at our door – Jack had recently left for the cabin and I was closing the gallery, packing to follow him. Our son and his partner were having problems and he needed refuge, for several reasons. I won't go into the details, but his words and deeds made a profound impact upon me, and I went, pretty much into tail-spin mode, because of what we, *then*, believed was a 'correct' sense of right and wrong action. I understand, now, that 'right' and 'wrong' are only words. We each have our own path to walk, and we can only walk ours – no one else's…no matter how much we Love them. We walk alone.

Wow, I always did say Chris has been my best teacher, in so many aspects of my spiritual life. He was and he still is.

After he left, I called Jack. Jack says this to me - "Barb, all the stuff I should have dealt with in my life, and didn't, all that stuff is all walking around in Chris." We were both sobbing.

I'd found out that day, my screenplay *14 Inches* had progressed into the semi-finals of an important script competition (no, I didn't win). The script is about an egocentric has-been basketball player turned newscaster, who offends a midget Haitian voodoo woman, who decides to teach him a lesson in humility, and she shrinks him down to 14 inches.

The fact that art (my script) was so painfully imitating real life wasn't lost on me. You may believe this, or not, but in a moment of extreme clarity, a voice began talking to me – dictating a book. I turned over the script (I'd been proofing it, again) and began writing exactly what the voice said – I wrote so fast and furious that, today, when I look at those pages, I can't even read them – completely illegible. That voice kept at me for over four years and often awakened me in the middle of the night, persistently talking and insisting I write down all it said, later to be typed. Now, it only speaks to me, intermittently. And I'm still typing - I have boxes and boxes of notes and transcripts.

So on that summer day, and as the fog curled up toward the cabin, the voice asked me to think about courage and it began telling me about true courage – the kind of courage Jack had, as he faced each and every moment of each and every day, without a drug or alcohol (which would certainly have dulled the pain of not feeling comfortable in his own skin, because of his genes) when every molecule, atom and cell in his brain and body must surely have cried out for just those very things. More importantly in this moment, today, the kind of courage you must have had, and have still, as you live through the challenges Cameron, and you, face on a daily basis.

The voice asked me to think about *real* courage – not the heroics of saving someone from a burning house – of course that's a definite kind of courage, but, rather, walking through each day of life and facing each situation immersed in Love and tenderness for Cameron, well, that is courageous to the nth degree.

My brother was merely six years old when polio attacked, and he ended up in an iron lung. I was but three and acutely aware that he was gone. He had a dozen operations by the time he left for college: skipped two grades, and was fairly young, as I recall.

Having Bubba as my brother gave me a unique perspective on courage, so when the voice spoke about it and I wrote about it, it was always the daily, moment-by-moment courage I focused upon and admire so profoundly. *You* simply see it as Love, in action, and it <u>is</u> that, of course. But as you spoke about what you'd gone through, I felt the terror you successfully battled. What could possibly be more frightening than watching your child get hurt and diminished and not being able to do anything? Nothing.

So, the voice reminded me of the depth of Love involved with genuine courage, and how to recognize it, in others. I had addressed you like this, previously:

"Dear NT, Gosh, now you're my hero; on a couple levels. I can't believe you slogged thru that letter. Yes, *letter* is a far better word."

I said it, somewhat teasingly, because I actually didn't think you'd taken the time to really read that silly odyssey I emailed you, but also to let you know that I do, indeed, put you up on my "Hero Pedestal" because of your physical prowess and daring. Now, as we share these experiences that we don't *have* to share, but *choose* to share and our friendship peels away another layer of protective ego, in order to expose our Spirits/Love (ie WHO WE ARE) and really share, well, you have polished another facet in your diamond, my Dear One. 'Hero' befits your spirit so very well.

My thoughts and Love are with you and your family. I intuitively knew, yesterday afternoon, things had not gone as you'd hoped, but to hear it from your very lips, sparked a brief sadness – I say brief, because I genuinely

37

believe all is well and, although you can't see into the future and know Cameron will find what he needs, he will. Truly. And I felt your Love and faith across the miles, which separate us. I felt *you*. You have a fine, deep Love and I Love it when I get to know people like you: it inspires me to be better than I ever thought I could possibly be. So, a courageous hero on several levels. Your family, too.

The fog? Yeah, I wrote and wrote and wrote, intermittently looking up, in awe, as it slowly rolled toward me. I thought about going inside and starting a fire – it was getting damp and cold – chilly to my bones. But I did not move; I just kept transcribing what the voice said. Finally, the voice quieted, and I put down my pen and released the stress and tension, which had bound my shoulders as I'd scribbled, concerned I might miss a word.

I stood and gazed toward the now hidden four mountain ranges, normally visible. The fog had accelerated and was moving more purposefully in my direction. Standing ground, I waited. Quickly, it advanced and moved onto the porch. I tore off my blue jean shirt, threw open my arms and my head back and laughed: it seeped into me, washed over me and I completely opened to it. I felt like what I imagine a flower must feel like as the morning dew settles and glides into every pore. It was exhilaratingly beautiful! It was one of the most heavenly sensual experiences I've ever had – me and the fog. Go figure.

Sometimes, in surrender, as in battle, we warriors can discover immense perfection. Joy. Wonder. Most of the time, we are heroes when we simply live; we navigate what the universe presents, in Love.

I Love you. I see the God-in-you.

Bright Blessings,
BHH – EMAIL - AFTER PRETTY HEAVY
TALK/FEB/NT CONVERSATION

Comfort in the Night: May 30, 1971
by
Barbara Helvey-Hughes, 1975

I recall love's knife edged night
When I just couldn't play it right
My youth stretched taut, my youth wrapped tight
Lithe life and light abandoned.

Dismayed, I marched away - alone
Watched promise bite to bold bare bone
Scarred glance and guile turned quick to stone
I shrugged on sweet, sweet sorrow.

Hushed angel's wings tore overhead
I disregarded where they fled
My wounds pumped hard, my wounds screamed red
And coursing, never faltered.

I sprinted, wild, through brittle years
Grief's heart tears glued to my eye's tears:
Transparent pearls, translucent fears
All wound and bound together.

My good intentions limped t'ward hell.
Clearly, my God knew me well.
My stalwart warriors cringed and fell.
I shuddered at their echo.

And standing, now, in middle age
Still striking blows against my cage
Could I, then, know the war I'd wage
Was all in all my making?

Emotion's motion – spinning spokes:
Will I outlive love's caustic jokes?

My words burn brave,
My words burn bright:
I seek no comfort from the night.
I take no comfort from the night.

I find no comfort, in the night.

2011/FL HOME/OBIT - E. FODOR: Awakened this
morning after you visited my dream: thought something was
wrong and got on Google. Broke down and wept when I
saw you'd left. I could feel your sorrow, Eugene. I
remember when you called me after I sent you that letter,
well, sent it to your parent's house out in Beaver Creek,
wasn't it? I still have their address – you told me to always
keep it: that was where you flew, when your wings got
singed. I was so damn happy to hear your voice, but I
knew, then, that all was not well for you, in this skin. Jack
saw the article in the Cape Cod Times I think, around 1989
or so...I couldn't believe it, because I knew for a fact that
you didn't so much as take a toke when you were first chair
at Indiana, Bloomington.

I'm so sorry I couldn't be there more, for you, but you
know I was loaded down with Jack and Jack's issues and
one of those was you and any other guy I knew, well,
forever. When we hung up, I realized I would never see
you again, in this life. My heart broke – shattered – I hate
the sound of breaking glass, and we all have those glass
hearts, don't we? Things are never easy, are they, but they
sure can be interesting and moving, beautiful: you were all
those, Eugene.

I still see you, in 1976, when I ran into you in Cincinnati, and you asked me backstage after your performance. I keep trying to recall that hotel, some grand old Dame. Netherland Plaza? I sat at the bar, you passed, saw me out of the corner of your eye, and we reconnected: was I looking for you?

I went to the concert and backstage. I remember *you*. See you in the next life.
BHH/ FADED DIARY PAGE, CRINKLED WITH A ZILLION DRIED TEARS

1975/MCGRAW-HILL CORPORATE OFFICES/AVENUE OF THE AMREICAS – 6ᵀᴴ AVE: Did I just get that job?! Yes! I catch a cab and head for Bloomingdale's – why? When I was sixteen years old, Mom took me shopping for my signature fragrance: a perfume I could wear, which everyone would associate with me and only me. I chose *L'Heure Bleue* by Guerlain and I've worn it all the ensuing years. Anyhow, I wanted genuine perfume, not cologne and I knew Bloomies had it. The depth of this scent – the initial, or top notes/the middle, or heart, notes/the base, or for me, called root, notes all combine to knock me out. I've worn it exclusively all my adult life.

L'Heure Bleue was created in 1912 by (Prince) Jacques Guerlain, infamous perfumer; its notes include bergamot, aniseed, carnation, orange blossom, heliotrope, Bulgarian rose, tuberose, iris, vanilla and musk. The very first store I headed to, on my very first trip to Paris, was Guerlain on des Champs-Elysees. It was a feast for all the senses. I left, having paid an outrageous amount of hard-earned money for the privilege of purchasing my favorite perfume from the originator. Worth every penny; the very experience lifted me closer to my version of heaven.

I love drinking Earl Grey tea, specifically because of the bergamot, so I find a cannibalistic element to this fragrance – a wanting, a needing to consume it on every possible level and in every possible way. Aniseed, which I truly do not like when served as licorice, but which I crave when used as a flavoring in other savory food, is in there… go figure. The flower notes compose the heart of this fragrance, but must be blended with everything else or we wouldn't have this amazing scent to begin with, right? Musk has never been, on its own, a keeper for me and yet, I know that without its sensual, shadowy, blue depth, *The Blue Hour* would be a very different perfume. Same with vanilla.

Maxfield Parrish painted the best representation of the Blue Hour, in several of his works – *Twilight* was one of them. The slow, constant seeping of soulful blue as all the colours fade and, finally, disappear.

It's the last thing our brains want light to do: vanish. Yet we gather at that exact hour, all over the world to witness the fading of the light. It provokes a melancholy, an almost "I don't believe what I just saw" sense of wonder, awe; this constant, daily repetition of the fading of the light…MacLeish was right – the 'shadow of the night' comes on quickly, almost imperceptibly. Fast. Blink, and you miss all its wonder, all the glory associated with the dying of the light…yes! That's what it is – we watch light die and then resurrect the following morning.

That's the wonder: our compulsion to understand mysteries. It's the underlying element of why *L'Heure Bleue* remains so enigmatic. It cannot be explained, nor can it be truly, understood. Funny how a perfume from childhood can possess such a lingering allure.

Many of my friends understand *L'Heure Bleue* is my signature fragrance and, if they know I'll be attending some event or function, they refrain from wearing it. As I would honor them, if I knew they wore a favourite.

I stood behind a former Love and waited for him to stop working on a computer, at IU, years after I graduated. Newly sober, I had amends to make. He stopped and cocked his head, stood, and turned around, saying, "Barb, I'd know that fragrance anywhere…" That's the point. BHH/1982/AFTER AMENDS TO DICKIE/IU/WATCHING & WAITING.

LATER/SAME DAY/2016: Namaste, Dear One. As I awakened just now, (6:45am) I was thrilled to see the sky already light. I've survived the long, dark nights of winter, in large part, thanks to you. I wasn't certain when I returned to Florida, how these past few months would play out. I mean, who can possibly know stuff like that? I do possess a deep and pretty complex sense of intuition, but I can't read the future. (Usually…)

In the mountains, before I came back South, my instincts screamed for me to cut and run, anywhere, and I haven't been a 'runner' (as in bailing out of painful, uncomfortable situations) for years. Generally, I see things through to the end - or to some kind of conclusion. That fear, that sense of urgency I used to feel, when I was younger and starting to feel trapped or confined in some way, starting to feel too alone or too not alone or well: pretty much *too anything*...returned.

I did manage to keep it under wraps, control it, push it down, pay it no mind, as in ignore it; but it's still buried deep, deep inside. (Inside that barrow, that tomb.)

43

I told you last eve about my new friend, that's her last name (Barrows) she's the one I shared a life with and when I heard her last name, I shivered: it's a word I used in the writing of one of my favourite poems and it means burial place, in my poem; as well as a container for grain. Seeds of a life, eh? Or a burial place for a love not lived, a frustrated love, a promise unfulfilled...that's what the poem is about, and it takes place in the late 19th century.
BHH/WOW – HOW DID I ARRIVE *HERE?*/EMAIL

2016/BOCA GRANDE, FL: Jack's gone and I'm not floundering as much as I was and that's because I'm here, where I'm surrounded by folks who love me and whom I love.

Jack told me I would have to get used to my 'new situation'. Yeah. Right.
I know, I know – everything's fuckin' perfect huh?
BHH/ON FIRE, AGAIN/NOTE IN DIARY

2008/CLYMERS, IN/LAST SUMMER WITH MOM/THINKING ABOUT LOVE/THINKING ABOUT AUNT LUCY: Mom's been really sick and I'm here for several months to help her and Dad. Kitty-corner across from my parent's farm sits my great-grandparent's home; a stately house (the Big House) dating to the beginning of the 20th century and where my Great Aunt Lucille lived and died.

I'm restless. I know Mom is in Trouble and I'm helpless to help my Dearest Friend in the world. All I can do is be here with her and try to make her days comfortable and peaceful. She falls asleep on the sofa a lot. I get squirrely and wander out to the front porch, where I stare at the Big House, a place I treasured as a kid – it was full of Treasure. And it always sparked my imagination.

44

'Aunt Lucy' was what we called her, since "great-aunt Lucy" would've been a mouthful for young mouths: she was a spinster. But I remember asking Mom if Lucy was ever sweet on anyone and Mom said 'yes' she was sweet on George T, who lived down the road in the hamlet of Clymers.

Years ago, you could see Lucy marching along the side of the curve, around and into the straight away and everyone knew she was going to see George. She walked like a soldier on a forced march, in her sturdy (almost combat boot-looking) shoes. Staring straight ahead.
If you honked or waved at Lucy, she simply ignored you.

Years later, in college, I too loved those sturdy combat-looking boots. I still wear them.

She was probably the wealthiest woman in the county. You'd never know it. She might have owned two, possibly three, dresses. She helped our family, immensely, after my brother got polio. She was often on my mind, as I sat there that summer with Mom.

This poem is for her and what I envisioned as her lost Great Love.

No Trace, Clymers, Indiana, 1916 by Barbara Helvey Hughes

When the lantern of night bit into dark
When the silver moon's teeth tore at the plain
When gravel shivered in the farmer's lane
And the skin on the trees wrinkled to bark
When the only sound was the moaning train
We met in the orchard by the shadowing oak.

I remember the words you almost spoke
With the harvest moon suspended above
And the bones of the earth rumbling below.
The sky archer readied his golden bow
And quieted coos of the grey-winged dove.
And we wrapped ourselves in the mourning cloak.

Those unspoken words will never be found -
Gone, forever, flew our promise of grace.
As I watched love's moment drain from your face
And the charge of your heart slip to the ground
Turned down with the reaping, leaving no trace
Then I knew your intent in my marrow.

Thrust like a pike, drove your gilded arrow.
I've trod these years on the hem of my life
Ignoring the pain which flows through my veins
Washed each autumn by the razoring rains
Wounding my soul like a riveting knife
To the still pumping heart of a sparrow.

I tender my fields; I lay down new seeds.
I work through the day and deep into night
Never accustomed to the bitter blight
Which gnaws at my farm, where the moontorch bleeds.
My orchard stands dead, but the bold oak's might
Continues to draw slow sap to the leaf.

Silent and broken I bury my grief
Out where the blanching moon tears at the plain.
Under the argentine light of the stars
I mound up the earth, which mimics my scars.
I cull the chaff from my barrow of grain
Alert to the absence of my heart's shadow thief.

2016/ECHOES OF 1971 - 45 YEARS LATER

I can hardly believe it. Thought my own urgency was long gone. It's funny (as in odd): I've been sensing it for the past couple years. Been feeling like I just needed to leave, to bail out, to skedaddle, to have an adventure, some freedom, a surety (is there such a thing?), a sense I am, indeed, still alive in this skin, in this moment, in this time and place. I've been a caregiver for decades and, maybe, it's wearing on me.

You know I've told you I do not feel isolated or alone, much, since I've been that monk and that warrior: warriors never feel alone and I guess monks don't either. I know they don't. But God, I just want to reach for you, Declan, and have you love me. I do feel that aloneness *right now*. Will I find you?

I have been stitched up with the threads of sorrow, this life. I hunger for serenity, and I ache for a profound sense of happiness. I grieve for peace, for contentment, for that which I do not seem to possess. Fulfillment must simply mean feeling full: completely full in every way and in every sense of the word. I would love it; perhaps I need it.

Usually I'm perfectly fine feeling a sense of wanting...it's sortof like suffering - a small dose can be a good thing, at times; but no, suffering is not 'above' as Antonio Porchia says, not always. Nothing is always anything...everything changes. And, no, I'm not in the throes of a mid-life crisis. There's just a stirring inside me, a yearning to be filled with life and to live. I've been feeling joyful and alert and aware and connected, because I've met incredible souls this year. Having Jack depart is made less painful. I feel an intense sense of gratitude. but, well...I do wanna meet you in Paris....

I love you, and that won't change; it's certain and immutable through all times, all places, all spaces, all everything. Warp speed and tracking beams engaged.

All that is missing is you, here. I know I "shouldn't," say that, but I did.

(I'm grateful I played out this hand, this time. Some hands just don't get played, or they get played badly. Never have been very good at bluffing – when you wear your heart on your sleeve, everyone can see it and those drops of blood leave a mean trail.)
Love and Brightest Blessings,
Barbara
BHH/EMAIL/SMOKIN'/SMOKIN'/SMOKIN':
PUKING OUT WORDS

MAY 30, 1976/MY 25TH BIRTHDAY: Feel odd this morning. My birth, and I have a strong sense of trepidation about this day, but no way I can cancel my plans. Taking Professor _____ to a Reds game and then out for a pizza. Going to pitch a proposal for his psych book – a writing schedule – and see where it goes.

I've been up since the wee hours, because I'm absolutely 'buzzing' – feels as if every cell in my body is vibrating. I usually only experience this sensation after I've driven a long distance, a long time. Must be the stress of traffic and being so 'on'/so alert. Anyhow, that feeling of effervescing keeps jumping all around me this morning. But I haven't driven anywhere, recently, so this is something else entirely. Premonition?

I am acutely familiar not only with The Blue Hour, but also, with the Midnight Hour, the Witching Hour(s), the Black of Night Hour, the Dead Dark Hour, the Hush of Night. Because those hours are the hours when I'm up and thinking of Declan, I'm writing my dream threads and re-membering those past lives, people, places. Was it only five years, today? He still has my heart. But I'm afraid to look for him.

Those of us who awaken for whatever reasons – like the wolf in bed, not alone, but, yes, alone, intimately know the Dead of Night. Every creak, each hum of an appliance coming on, juice pumping through the wires; all those inconsequential sounds not even noticed in the light of day when all those same sounds jump and grind and murmur and thrum, slicing the silence; yeah, we know those, we know that time, those moments, those sounds, that uneasy feeling when we'd rather be outside with Nature's unknown forces than inside with manmade ones. Ghosts in the machines again. Robots readying to revolt.

So that's how this day started. This day, which should carry some kind of importance, because, well, I'm now a quarter century old. Hate it when that happens…things have shifted…I have shifted. SHIFT/SHIFT/SHIFT/END OF MESSAGE

I sense a nanosecond *time* shift. That's what's going on - I know what will happen a nanosecond before it actually <u>does</u> happen. I know the phone will….there it goes. I already know who it is and don't care to chat with them, so I shine that one on. Grab my briefcase, purse, and head out. I'm meeting him at the stadium, so yeppers, Red Ryder. Let the games begin.

The X-1/9 whines into the stadium lot and I get a great spot. Feeling pretty darn good as I jump out of the car and head toward my meet.
BHH/JOTTED ON MCGRAW HILL
STATIONERY/DATED MAY 30, 1976

MAY 30, 1971/BLOOMINGTON: WOW! What just happened? I'm back at IU - Declan and I just made love/had sex/fucked! WOW! I feel the Love Vibe, seriously. That was awesome and the best freakin' thing I ever experienced!

We laugh so hard I begin feeling giddy – not sure I can even get out of bed. I didn't know you were a virgin, says Declan. I gaze (yeah, *gaze)* into his eyes. Man, I swear I get lost in there. Getting lost seems to be a pattern with me.

LATER: Why all the watching? says I. Joe, says he...I knew he had you in his sights, too. I laugh. There are probably 30,000 students on this campus, says I and you're telling me you knew Joe has a thing for me? Yeah, I know he does, says Declan, and he doesn't deserve you. He's a user and, I love...Yeah? says I. Nada.

He says he loves me, says I. When? asks Declan. Christmas, says I...he told me he's never told a girl he loves her, before...You believe him? says he. Don't think so, says I...you're right - he's a user, that's what I'm thinking. He's full of anger and negative stuff and I don't trust him.
You shouldn't trust him, says he.
How do you know him? says I.
We just met...not friends, says Declan.
Wanna tell me something? says I.
Not right now, says he. How'd you know him?
He kept leaving notes under my wiper blades, says I.
What kinda notes? says he.
Sort of threatening notes: they all said something like 'I'm watching you' or 'I'm following you', says I. That bastard, says he. Is he still doing that?

Naw, he stopped when he found out I work at Fred's, says I. He comes in a lot. Declan shakes his head, narrows his eyes.

You know, he was in Viet Nam, says I.
I know — that's where he became an addict, says he.
Addict? says I. Yeah, heavy into heroin, says he. How would you <u>know</u> that? says I.

I'm thinking, to myself…well that answers a lot of questions. Addict….no wonder he's jumping around like a teardrop on a hotplate! No wonder he's angry.

You think his family knows?
Why do you think his folks keep such a tight rein? says he. Has his mom contacted you? No, says I.

Less than a year later, she would be returning the letters I wrote to JFC — opened — and telling me Joe can't be in touch with me, thus breaking my heart; mostly for him. But, then, I knew I couldn't save him…all I can do to try and save myself.
BHH/*MEMORIES* WRITTEN IN CURSIVE ON BARBARA A. HELVEY STATIONERY, DATED 1988 WITH A NOTE: JFC RUNS AA MEET IN LOGAN? LIVES THERE???

MAY 30, 1976/CINNCINATI REDS STADIUM/ OH: Okay, this has just been almost too weird. I ask a question and immediately already know what he's going to say, in return. I feel like my brain's stuttering!
BHH/DIARY NOTE/DATED 1976

MAY 30, 1971/MAY/BLOOMINGTON, IN: and I've just been laid for the very first time and it was amazing. We shower, get dressed and head out. He puts an overnight

51

bag in my trunk. We drive around, get supper, go to a baseball game – a local game, maybe junior high school, over by the RCA factory (more on that, later).

Dark, and Declan says, I need you to take me somewhere and I follow his directions: over by Kirkwood Ave., we pull into a large house's parking lot – probably a rooming house. Declan retrieves the bag from the trunk. I'll be back in a jiffy, says he. It's later than dusk and there are no lights around the house, but I can make him out, as he heads toward it. Am I seeing things? I wonder, as I think I see Declan scale up the side of the house to the second floor and enter through a window!

A few minutes later, I'm squirming in my seat, wondering what the heck is going on, when he returns with a briefcase, gets in and drops the briefcase between his feet.
Whaddya doin'? says I. Business says he. Now, I'm uneasy. Let's go home, says he. I kick it into gear and the MG scampers away. What's going on?
BHH/POSS CHAPTER BOOK – *PATTERNS*, 2014.

1983/ANNAPOLIS, MD: Mom, says I, today I saw the man I'm gonna marry. Marry? says Mom. Really? What's his name? I don't know his name, Mom, I just <u>saw</u> him. Oh, you won't believe this! Just in time – my biological clock's ticking away.
BHH/ALWAYS/ALWAYS/ALWAYS/I BELIEVE EVERYTHING/HARTBREAK NOTES

2016/BOCA GRANDE, FL: Wow…doctrine and dogma and I can't seem to persuade him past this stuff he's been carrying around since he was a good kid, going to parochial school. When they get us to the point where we stop thinking and only recite, they know they'll survive another day.

I wonder why it's so hard to believe we are each God. Why, so easy to believe Jesus was the Son of God and we are not...doctrine and dogma. Who ever thought it would persist through all these intervening centuries? When we all decide to accept that we ARE God and God dwells within each of us and all we have to do is believe and act upon those beliefs...well, okay, we'll probably explode and shoot home. Gloria in excelsis Deo. Pax, brother.
BHH/PRACTICING LATIN/MY LIFE WITH JACK BOOK

1980/ANNAPOLIS: Rowing today on the Severn. Meeting at St. John's boathouse. Love doing this, but traveling so much leaves me little time to do these things I truly enjoy. There are also four of us, who decided to start a Women's art group: LA, Sigrid T, Sandy K, and me. We'll be doing exhibits in DC and maybe around here, too. It's great to make friends with these talented women...LA is the key, here, and I know we've lived a life or two together, for sure.
BHH/LOST IN WONDER WITH THE GIRLS IN THE BOAT...

1994/TILGHMAN ISLAND, MD.: Storms have been ravaging our shoreline and it's a mess out there. Jack squirreling around and wants to go to Florida, on a fishing trip. I say okay. He doesn't need my okay. He left and there's finally peace in our beautiful home.

Chris and I watched the snowfall last night; made torches, lit them about midnight and marched down past the Bean's house to wander around on the vacant lot, down by the water, where all the pine trees grow. We searched and searched for the fairies: you know, the ones who use those huge toadstools in the summertime, to lay out their bounty and share din-din with each other. Around 1am, we made snow angels, since the unexpected snow was so deep, tromped home and snuggled up to a fire in the family room.

I made us hot chocolate and we watched *It's a Wonderful Life*. Chris fell asleep with his head in my lap on the pillow I made for him when he was five years old – cowboys and injuns.

God, thank you for this soul. He is amazing and as long as he lives a full life, I will be Grateful.
BHH/ON THE BACK OF MY NEW SCRIPT – *THE GOLDEN THREAD* – UPLOADED ON AMERICAN ZOETROPE, TODAY

1987/APPROX. NOT SURE OF YEAR/TILGHMAN ISLAND/SHIPWRIGHT'S COVE:
This morning Scooter (Chris) sauntered (yeah, really) into our room. He's about two and a half.

This life's much nicer than that last one, says he. You know, Mommy, that last life I had.
I startle.
What life, Scooter, asks Jack.
It wasn't very happy. This one is much better, says Scooter.

I want more, but Scooter clamps his mouth shut and just won't give us anything more than he already did…and, isn't that just the way of it, *always*?!
You want more and they let you starve to death.
BHH DIARY DATED 1990

1989/TILGHMAN ISLAND: Why is Jack so incredibly uncomfortable in his skin this time? It makes my life with him so unpredictable and uneasy. I never know where he's coming from or where he's headed and I yearn for him to be with me.

54

He reminds me of JFC, Jr. so very much. Guess addicts are all pretty much driven by the same desires – jumping out of your skin takes a lot of thought, time, and effort.

I wish he'd just calm down, relax, and enjoy the time we have this time. Who knows how long it will be before we share another life or, even, IF we'll ever share another life. Can't count on it and better make the most of it, while it's here.

Damn, there are times I surely do miss him. Weeds abound. Don't know what to do.
BHH/DOES NOT COMPUTE/DOES NOT COMPUTE/DOES NOT COMPUTE

2015/AUGUST 25/CABIN/BLUE RIDGE MTS., NC:
Good thing A. is here.
A. did all the prep work for tonight's Mexican meal, last night, so we can go to Blowing Rock and check out a new restaurant, then scope out the shops. I love taking her shopping and spending time with her.

We left early. I kissed Jack goodbye around 8am. A. and I headed out and were excited about doing some exploring – we went to a potter's studio, yesterday, and I got A. a beautiful pot, then on to a couple other potters and she's now got a good start on a fine Blue Ridge Mountains pottery collection.

Heading out to Blowing Rock, where we shared a fantastic lunch of fresh mountain trout, which was just wonderful – everything was great and A. kept saying how she wished Uncle Jack were with us. Me, too. She was toting my heavy purse and a brass fixture broke. I startled, because I was having a very weird feeling. Brushed it away and said Don't

55

worry, Jack can fix it. A few seconds later another brass fitting on the strap broke. I looked at A., my brain racing. We've got to get home, now! says I.

When we returned home to the cabin and I raced into the bedroom to give Jack the t-shirt I got him, but I'd already felt his absence all the way home. The purse was simply his way of saying I'm leaving. Jack was warm, but had definitely left the cabin. WOW – I am so freaked out and not much freaks me out anymore: usually just Loved Ones, in trouble…well, he's not in trouble, now. He's fine. I'm the one who's going to have a hard time with this. He was just telling me, a couple weeks ago, that he hoped I'd go to Ireland for the trip we planned, if he left first.

I didn't feel his energy anywhere when we got home to the cabin and, although I knew he was nowhere around, I just couldn't process that my husband was gone. He left without saying goodbye. But I knew he would. When he recently asked me to promise I wouldn't put him on life support, I could not promise. I jokingly told him he'd better die when I was gone because I am <u>never</u> gone and we're always together. Why didn't I see this coming?

He did just that.
POOF!

Last evening, A. asked Jack to join us on the front porch for the sunset. Jack and I have seldom missed watching the sunset together, until this summer. He's very sick and he sleeps nonstop. I can't seem to entice him out and that concerns me, deeply. But he got out of bed and came out, after supper, and we all chatted and laughed. He told A. Barb and I are proof positive that you can fall in love with someone and, thirty-three years later, love them even more than when you met them. Those words both humbled and touched me. I sure wish he'd said those words years ago. He rarely gave me a clue as to how he genuinely felt about anything.

As the sun dove westward and splashed washes of orange, violet and yellow over the blue, blue, Carolina blue, he put his arms around me and kissed me. Says I love you, Sweetheart. I'm tired. Think I'd better lay down – that new medicine makes me so tired I can hardly believe it. I'm sorry, A., I gotta go back to bed.

He headed away. Back to bed. How terrible. Later, a raging nosebleed and I ask him to let me take him to the emergency room. He says no. He has doc appt. next week and the bleed is because it's so dry in the cabin.

Today, Jack's gone. I'm reeling.

Hartbreak…heartbreak.
BHH/MARCH 2016/PLACIDA, FL/BARELY LEGIBLE DIARY ENTRY

1980/ANNAPOLIS, MD: I've met some great people and my friend, LA feels so amazingly familiar. Feel time-warped, like I just met a soul from many of my journeys. We will become great friends in this life. She looks so much like him, she could be Declan's sister. Weird.
BHH/THINGS TO REMEMBER/JOTTED IN ON A NOTEBOOK PAGE:
WHO WERE WE, AS MONKS???
DARRAGH (oak) (pr. Derr-a) AND CAHIR (warrior) (pr Kaw-heer)?
BHH/THAT'S MY HUNCH

1972/OCTOBER/BLOOMINGTON, IN: Home early from an all-nighter. Stopped in the health food store on

Kirkwood and someone approaches me from behind and loops their arm through mine, I spin around and find myself staring up and into those green, green eyes. Declan, why can't you release me? Cut to the other side of the street if you see me. Please stop this nonsense.

How've I been?! I haven't seen him for months and, now, suddenly, there he is: here I am.
God, how I love him. Will this ever end? Can we stop loving the ones who journey so far with us?
Is that even *possible*? I feel as if someone has kicked me in the guts and I'm trying my best just to breathe, right now.

Walk you home? says he.
Better not, says I. He releases me. Pulls me back toward him and holds me, right there: heart to heart. I love the way he smells. I love him. I will always love him, but can we be together, this time? Reminds me of our paths a thousand years ago, in Ireland. What the?! Where'd that come from?!
Where ya living? says he.
Naaa, we better not, says I.
He smiles that crooked smile and I ask, Where you living?
With _____, couple blocks from here, says he. Pain shoots across my face. He leans in and whispers: Remember, you left me, Barbara, not the other way around.
Well, says I, that's not *entirely* true, now, is it?
I thought you were coming down, when I called at the end of summer, says I.
I did and you weren't there, says he.
MG broke down and I did my best to get here. Why didn't you wait? says I.
You were talking in drunk riddles, says he. You wanna clarify, now?
No, says I, you know the bones of it, (me, knowing it's too late and I have a lot of school to make-up). Besides, he's doing something, and I doubt he'd get it, even now.

Mom said you called my house on August 5th, says I.

I had a feeling; says he and I was concerned about you –
thought something was terribly wrong. It was that, wasn't
it? says he.

You don't even know the worst of it, and I don't feel like
sharing, right now, says I. I just can't…. Anyhow, if you
knew, why not wait?

Wish I had, says he, but I can't go back, can I? I <u>do</u> love
you he murmurs – so, so much.

….and I walk away from, possibly, the deepest love of my
all-time existence, for the, God-only-knows how many
times so far, in this life and possibly in others….no wonder
I will continue to feel such a thorough void even decades
later. Why is it so hard to release our egos and tell our
Truth?

Are you The One, Declan? Events seem to, so far, conspire
to keep us apart. Will we end up together? Don't
know…..you don't need to know this, yet…….

I'm dying here and I know ….pretty much…..nuthin'….

BHH/1972/IN OMAR KHAYYAM'S *THE RUBAIYAT*
DIARY, BDAY GIFT FROM LISA

1981/ANNAPOLIS. MD/EASTPORT: Sis and I sit at the
bar, Marmaduke's, having drinks. Sitting next to Sis is a
man, who looks intensely familiar, and his energy is popping
all over the place as he glances, repeatedly, at me. I smile.
He's trim and very tall and has the most beautiful eyes, but
it's dark and I can't see their colour. I'm working in college
publishing and haven't, yet, joined AA. This encounter
might just be one of the compelling reasons I eventually did.

Geez, do I know this guy?! He keeps riveting those eyes on
me, I glance at him and his eyes dart away. I lean forward,
aghast and whisper to Sis: Oh my God, I think that's Declan
Niall!

Who is Declan Niall? says she.

That guy, you know, from IU – the one – my *first*!!!!! Wow, says I, he's so…well…preppy! Doesn't look sick and doesn't look like a hippie. He was sick and looked like a well-worn hippy/addict last time I saw him.

Oh, says she…holy shit….you wanna change seats and sit next to him??? Says she.

Shhhhhhh, says I. He cocks his head and hears. Reaches into his pocket, throws a bill on the counter and, abruptly, scrambles off the bar seat and out the door: NO WAY JOSE!!!!!! We follow. Quick, like bunnies.

Are you sure it's him? says she. Abso-fuckin-lutely, says I.

Hey, Declan, I call. He stops. Turns around and we face one another. You have me confused with someone else, says he, and he practically runs toward a huge sailboat, where I see someone waiting.

What the F was <u>that</u>?!

In the end, we're all whores, aren't we?

BHH/HOPPIN' DOWN THE BUNNY TRAIL AND LOSING MY – Whatever/MIND/WAY???/2016

1990/TILGHMAN ISLAND, MD.: LA arrives the day after Jack takes off to do some shows in Florida and get in some fishing. The winter storms battered the shoreline and threw up all kinds of treasures for us to discover. Scoot's been out there scavenging for days. IIt's Christmas break.

I'm always so happy to spend time with LA. Not only is she the dearest, kindest friends I've ever been blessed with, but she also keeps me posted on all my Annapolis friends on the Western shore. Our conversations leave few stones unturned.

This time we're talking about the possibility of past lives – for real or not? I say yes. Chris' (Scooter's) comments, as a child just learning to speak in complete sentences, have been a definite influence on both me and Jack – when he told us that this life was much nicer than his last life, we couldn't figure out where the comment came from, if not from actual experience....he was so young he had no chance to hear something like that and he was too young to even process such a comment. Since then, I've learned a lot about research conducted by Ian Stevenson and others and children with past life experiences.

Anyhow, back then, I told LA from the very first time I met her there was a familiarity to her, which I couldn't put my finger on, but which I had experienced with many others, during this life. I'd come to believe these are souls I've known in other lives...she wasn't so sure.

I suggested we do an experiment, and I tore a sheet of paper in two and handed her half, asking her, "If you had lived another life, what do you think it was...if we shared that life?" We both wrote. I say, Let's read what each other wrote. We exchange papers.

Both of us wrote one word: monk

The funny thing was this – I'm a writer...all I ever wanted to be and what I believe I was meant to be – my 'vocation' if you will.

LA is an artist and had done a series of paintings – small works done in gouache, on paper – really lovely pieces, which reminded me of Persian carpets...I think those rugs inspired them, actually.

Now I'm flashing forward to 2016: MARCH 19th and I can't sleep so I get up to write. I know I'm gonna write about LA several times today and, just for the hell of it, I Google (can you believe that's a _verb_?!) *Book of Lindisfarne*, thinking I should order some books on illuminated manuscripts, because I've taken all mine to my NC studio…so, I do. As I'm deciding which books to get, I make a wonderful discovery - in a minute, I'll share it with you.

Back in 1990, LA and I just stare at each other when we unfold the papers and read the word "monk". I'm really excited and I see the whole thing crystal clear. Yes – she was the monk who did the illumination, and I was the monk, who copied the verse - totally made sense. We were best friends. Totally get it, now.

This morning as I'm browsing through the contents of those books, I discover that some of the illuminations in the Lindisfarne manuscript are called "Carpet pages" because of their resemblance to intricate Persian carpets…there are no co-incidences, but sometimes it takes a while to connect all the dots. If you can't see them, you can't connect them. Right? Right. BHH/BG, FL/HUGHES GALLERY

Monk Dreams by Barbara Helvey Hughes
Yes.
I remember the book.
My tiny, sunlit space
Some long-forgotten place
Of stone and night-hawk cave
Where evening's bleeding grace
Arced wide and blazoned high
Across the scarlet sky.
Yes.
I remember the book.

And how my bony fingers
Then armed with cartilage sword
Scratched the surface of the hoard.
And bright, those words still linger.
Yes.
I remember the book.
How years dropped down like thunder
Through dim sunlight in my cell
And I, shot through with wonder
Inked blank pages from the well.
Yes,
I remember the book.

I remember the book.

THURSDAY/JANUARY 28, 2016: Now I've reconnected with all of my Three. It was not necessary for me to touch any of them, in order to be aware of who they are to me and what they mean to me. They are my sacred three and the fact that they are all men and I, a woman, is simply the roll of the dice. I've met many, many important souls in this pivotal and key life, but Declan, Jack and NT are the three major players throughout my journey: my long, long journey. Sometimes we switch gender, sometimes we change roles, sometimes we share only a sliver of the current life – maybe when we do that, it's simply to reassure one another that we remember we are parts of our whole – I don't know the whys, whats, hows, wheres (mostly) and whens…I'm lucky to recall anything.

What do I do if there's more than Three? If nothing else, I've learned to roll with the punches, the surprises, situations, circumstances/etc/etc – thanks, Babe (Jack).

I imagine at times we have all been one another's moms, uncles, best friends, brothers, sisters, teachers, fathers, mentors, champions, defenders, baiters, enemies, well, you get the larger picture, right? Our roles change as our desires to grow into our spirits change.

I imagine myself as a rock and Jack as the stream rushing over me. I see Declan as the sun warming me in the high forest, where I'm an ancient sequoia. NT has probably been the mockingbird, singing its heart out in the tree next to Scooter's window, putting us to sleep each night and singing us awake each dawn. We must become what we need to become to get to the place we mean to be.

Sounds easy, but it is not. If one teeny, tiny thing had not occurred, if I'd not gone one place, you'd not met one other soul, neither of us been born at this time and in this place, if one thought had not raced through our minds, we would not have met. Everything must be perfect for all these things to happen. Everything IS perfect.

As I said, it was unnecessary for me to touch any of these spirits to know them, but when I did touch them, it was explosive. Even when I first hugged LA, Lisa, and Sharon etc., etc…my female friends: I knew I knew them from before and will know them, ever after. As soon as I had a visual on Jack, my brain went berserk: Fourth of July fireworks.

After I told Mom that I'd seen him, I'd been asked, by my friend, Sterling, to chair an NA meeting in Annapolis. I always chaired meetings on the topic of Gratitude. I couldn't believe it when Jack walked in. I couldn't believe it when Jack fell asleep about fifteen minutes into my talk. I still can't believe I was so naïve as to not understand that he was using.

There he was, again, when I chaired an AA meeting at the Red House in Annapolis the following week. He approached me after the meeting and introduced himself, volunteering to help me make frames for the paintings I'd just completed for my first upcoming one-woman art show in Annapolis.

I was ecstatic. The fact that I actually asked Jack to marry me, only a few days into our project, still freaks me out. I'm surprised that I ever even saw him again. But I <u>did</u> see him - we lived together, married, and had a child and stayed together for thirty-three years. That's the stuff of dreams and nightmares and just plain old life, unfolding before our eyes and everyone else's. That's the courage.
BHH/MEMORIES OF ANNAPOLIS AND MEETING/A QUARTER OF MY EQUATION

1984/ANNAPOLIS/EASTPORT/SEVERN AVENUE: How do we change our lives, our patterns? How do we stretch, rise, evolve? Do we always act without thinking or do we, once in a while at least, give consideration to our thoughts, our words, our actions? Maybe it's easier for some than others.

Our neighbor, Parker F., fell again today and I heard his wife Barbara screaming for Jack to come and help. I love the fact that he's always on the ready to help them. Jack and I love our neighbors and all I can hope is that there will be someone who loves us, when we're in our eighties or nineties, and who will come to our aid when we're in need.

Jack's so full of possibility and promise. It will be a huge feat if he can keep himself away from the drugs, though: I 'get' how he's genetically programmed, and I understand how difficult it must be for him. It's the pain, you know?

The physical pain. The mental and emotional pain. The Spiritual pain. Is there intellectual pain? Don't know, but all the pain we heap on ourselves and which everyone else heaps upon us, during every life, weighs us down. It takes a huge spirit to shift that pain off our shoulders and completely away from us.

I believe Jack possesses that huge spirit – I'm counting on it.

I've never known such a brilliant human as Jack, and because of my profession in college publishing, I've known some great and amazing minds. There's something different about Jack – it's not merely his intellect. It's <u>how</u> he learns, <u>how</u> he's so hands on and loves books and grabs ideas, almost out of thin air: out of his/our dreams. He's awake on every *organic* level.

But it's his Spirit I'm concerned about. He still hasn't worked through the 12 Steps. There's some deep fear in there and I think he might believe some of his behaviours are simply unforgivable. He's wrong. Nothing, absolutely nothing, is unforgivable.

Declan, I had to move forward. Jack needed me; you loved me, but did not need me and that makes all the difference - to me.

To forgive is huge – it's directly tethered to love and, so, must be in the 'key harmonic realm' of human behaviours. When Jack wants to show me something he either draws it or we put our foreheads together: touching foreheads is a custom among ancient peoples and Jack (Pathfinder) is Cherokee, Choctaw, Sioux (also, Norman French/English). I wish I could touch my forehead to his and let him see what I see, so he would be confident of his soul's path.

Everything is perfect – he just doesn't believe it and I can't do that, for him. Damn! It's always something!

I fell out of 10th century, IRE (as a male) and into 20th century USA (female). I'm certain there were other lives in between those two, but they were (are) significant ones. And, wow, I'm not sure which is worse – having to camouflage myself as in clothing, and attitudes (for the 10th century) or having to camo my spirit and mind (for the 20th...). When are we closer to God? Where? Do we ever realize just how close we are - and <u>that</u> we <u>are</u>?
BHH WRITTEN ON A SHEET OF PERSONAL STATIONERY AND TAPED TO THE END PAGES OF A REPLICA OF A SMALL, BEAUTIFUL ILLUMINATED MEDIEVAL PRAYER BOOK/DATED 1985, INSCRIBED 'PREGNANT WITH CHRISTOPHER BURLESON HAMPTON RYAN HUGHES'

2016/AFTER JACK: I've never felt so lost and so alone, or so relieved. What do I do when winter season ends and everyone leaves? Actually, I <u>have</u> felt this lost and alone; 1982-83, right before I met Jack, when I couldn't find Declan. Where do I go from here? I can't plan anything, Hartbreak. Thanks NT I needed you: you came through, as I knew you would. Dear One. Truly, you are that.…
BHH/WATCHING AND WAITING

1971/72?/BLOOMINGTON, IN: My hometown friend, Cathy (Cat) and I drive to IU for the weekend, because I returned too late to enroll, this semester, when my MG's clutch gripped and busted, right as that car rolled across the highway directly in front of me outside McKinney, Virginia and I had to stay in McKinney and wait for them to get and install a new clutch.

WHEW! At the garage I met a really great guy and we
stayed up all night talking – yeah, just talking: remembering
what the weeks before this drive home had wrought. I'm
saving his letter and will always remember him. He saved
my life. Lifesavers…First, angels saved me from getting
killed by the car flip/roll, then this total stranger.

Really, I thought I'd just crash and burn after DC and all
that - the fact that Declan was probably still in Marrakech
and I was in Bloomington made it all so surreal. This is
what he (the McKinney, VA guy) wrote to me in his letter:
"If you got it, don't lose it.
You got it, don't it lose you?
I have it, still. (the letter or 'it'?) He did what he said he
would do, which was to write to me and make sure I was
okay - just like NT did when Jack died.
BHH/FEELIN' GROOVY/FEELIN' LOVED

1971-72???/MONTHS AFTER THE MCKINNEY
CRASH: Cat and I are just getting ready to open the door of
Nick's Pub for a night of revelry and I'm hoping to see
some of my many friends, who did not, foolishly as I, miss
fall enrollment….when someone comes up from behind me
and wraps his arms around me, spins me around to face him
and I'm staring into those mesmerizing green eyes, again.
Cat giggles. Declan smiles his winning smile and looks her
up and down. Go on in, Cat, says I. She giggles, again and
sashays on in, to hoots and hollers. Those Bloomington
boys…

I try to squirm free and Declan tightens his hold, pulling me
closer. You always smell so awesome, says he. I wince. He
angles his head down to my neck and breathes, deeply.
God, you have this smell that I can't seem to get over, says
he, holding my gaze.

L'Heure Bleue, says I, wanting to melt – but I know if I do, I'll never finish college.

I pull away. Keep looking at him and know I'd better memorize his features, because one day I'll not be able to find him – yeah, intuitively, I knew that, right then - it's haunted me forever and back then, there were no easy-use cameras or camera phones.
Had to look, hard. Breathe, Barbara, breathe…

I smile at him and I'm overwhelmed with the desire to fall back into his arms and just leave with him, then I think about the immense pain I've walked through simply trying to forget him and move forward with my life. Gotta go, says I. I love you, says Declan. Me, too, says I and that's just so fuckin' sad…I enter Nick's and look away when he passes our table. His hand grazes my shoulder.
Goosebumps.

Wow, he's too cute, says Cat. I get the feeling you two belong together.

In another life, says I, and I know that's true, too. Many lives. That One…this one?

Mike C barrels in and asks to sit down – I shoo him away.
He turns back and says, You know he's crazy about you….
Is he sick? says I, concerned. He's lost a lot of weight.
Depends on how ya mean sick, says he. Doin' what he shouldn't be doin', Barb…and, lovin' you. From afar. Mike smiles and leaves.
What's he mean? says Cat.
I dunno, lied me.
BHH JOURNAL/1983/2016
FORTY-FIVE YEARS OF WATCHIN' AND
WAITIN'/WAITIN' AND WATCHIN'

BOCA GRANDE, FLORIDA/HUGHES
GALLERY/MARCH 2016: How do we manage to live, to
make it through our lives without the people we most love?
How do we successfully do anything when so many integral
spirits never connect with us in most of our existences?
How do we do it? We do it because we don't remember
much of it – if we did remember, we couldn't live. It's that
simple…we're walking blind and aren't even aware. Let
alone, awake. Look at me, I'm sort of aware and the
knowing just practically kills me on a daily basis.

Some folks must pray for amnesia. It's your party. Cry if ya
want to.
BHH/*PATTERNS*

1885/ANOTHER TIME/ANOTHER
PLACE/WESTERN NORTH CAROLINA – Who is that
guy, asks Eileen…do you know him? My eyes track a lean,
dark-haired man, who's in the middle of an intense fencing
match.
Yes, says I, smilin: I'll be back in a minute.
I rush off to a dressing room, where I don fencing gear.

Back at the match, Matt has bested his opponent, and I step
forward, en garde! Several parries and a couple lunges.
Quick steps back and forth. We cross swords, forearms
touching. I smile.
Murchad/Matt/NT says, Where you been? I smile, again,
because he recognizes me, my energy, immediately.

I'm, now, a male, recent Irish immigrant, living in Asheville,
North Carolina and I own a small publishing company
called *Golden Threads*. I always did say that although NT was
the one who, consistently, had the hardest time with all this

70

past-life stuff, once he figured it out, in whatever life he was in, and what we all mean to one another - he never faltered.
Hello, says I.
There you are, says he.
Here I am, says I. Eileen's bitin' at her bit. She remembers.

As luck would have it, he's a writer and he's made an appointment, with me, the following day, so…

Next day, as he's entering our offices, Eileen's about going crazy, because she has a chance, this time, and tells me she's never forgot him (as Murchad) when she (as Beircheart) fought beside him to protect me (as Mahon) back in the tenth century, Ireland.

I love how the universe always knows and looks out for us: you can call it chaos if you want. To me, it's perfection. God-in-us. That's what this is – it's all just God-in-Us.

Wish I had a chance, but I'm not cut that way, this time, so I say, 'Let him know'.
She smiles and says, I plan on it. She's such a warrior, in all of her lives (the ones we've shared anyhow), that I hope he survives his initiation!

But, yeah, he's got a clue and more than one, because he knew exactly who I was. Connecting those dots…ain't life crazy??? Which life? All?

Did you see that light flash, spin, and blaze across the sky last night? So fast, I could barely follow it and it did some right-angle turns I didn't think were possible, for shooting stars or meteorites. What the hell could that thing BE?! BHH/ASHEVILLE/FOUND IN A HANDMADE LEATHER JOURNAL, EMBLAZONED WITH THE ANCIENT TRIQUETRA SYMBOL, and signed in clear/legible cursive script "MAHON O'MATHGHAMHAIN, 1885"

CHAPEL HILL/NC/1979: Everything's important, everything possesses energy - people and places and things. I've started painting, again, but instead of oil, gouache, or watercolour, I'm trying a new medium called acrylic. It's a plastic derivative or something. It dries really fast and balls up into these tiny pieces of, well, plastic…really weird to work with, but water soluble so no fumes and as much as I love smelling those fumes, I know they really aren't all that good, especially in an enclosed space. The more I use it, the better I'll get. No more headaches.

Symbols are important. Lots of times when I read, I think in symbols…sometimes I figure it must be sort of difficult to be my friend, because I just don't process and translate like a normal person – wow, that either sounds incredibly arrogant, or stupid…not sure which.

Vassar Miller, the Texas poet I discovered back in the 1960's, wrote one of my favourite poems. The last line goes like this: "Praise Peter, who could weep his sin away/but never see me where I hang/huge teardrop on the cheek of night." (*Judas* by Vassar Miller, lines 12-14, from *My Bones Being Wiser,* 1963)

I was maybe twelve or thirteen, when I discovered this wonderfully graphic poet and became obsessed with rendering her words into images.

I saw, and still <u>see</u> Judas, hanging there, on night's plump cheek, right there, encased in that big ole fat teardrop. With a noose around his neck and me, standing below him, bawling my eyes out, because I know he (Judas) loved Jesus more than any of those others. Why do humans seem to

get it SO AMAZINGLY WRONG? Why were Jack's
Mom's last words to me, "We always take the wrong road."?

On February 1st, I went to a private clinic to fix a serious
sinus problem – or, so I was told and strangely a few hours
before the surgery, I fell asleep and had a dream – in the
dream I died. Bad omen? Warning?! DANGER, WILL
ROBINSON! DANGER!!!!

Later, during surgery, I somersaulted backwards off the
operating table, ending up in the top far corner where two
walls and the ceiling meet and gazing down at myself; on
the OP table, there I was, gushing blood all over the place.
A soft light warmed my back and a melodic voice asked me,
but not in words, if I wanted to stay or go. I answered, but
not in words, that my brother needs me so I'd best stay.

Next thing I know, I'm awakening post-op and can't see out
of my right eye and, although I can barely talk because there
is no saliva in my dry, dry mouth, I manage to communicate
to a nurse that I'd like her to remove the patch on my right
eye. She explains there is no patch over my eye and that it's
a side effect of the anesthesia.

I continue to complain as much as I'm able, but no one
cares, or listens, until Sis arrives and I'm crying, crying,
crying and she insists someone call doctors, but, of course,
it's too late and I'm permanently blind in my right eye, with
the possibility that I will, eventually, be completely blind,
should my left eye feel like joining the right, in sympathy: no
way!

Ain't gonna happen! Please, please, please tell me/show me
a sign/open the heavens and scream that I won't lose both!

PLEASE.

Okay....no word, no utterance, no signals or symbols so I'm packing my bags and I'm leavin' on a jet plane to see every freakin' painting I can see, before, or if I DO loose the other one. Eye, that is.

MONA, here I come!
BHH/MAY/1979/BOOKIN' IT/LITERALLY AND FIGURATIVELY/WRITTEN ON A LEGAL PAD AND THROWN IN A BOX, WITH A BUNCH OF OTHER LEGAL PADS

WINTER/1974/BLOOMINGTON, IN/DISCO CITY:
So, Dickie and I have been dating since autumn, 1972, after I returned to college and met him at a college bar, where I waitress. I am, finally, in love again. He's amazing, smart, sweet, handsome and he's very sensitive.

Mom and Dad have come and removed the distraction of my MG, but Dickie has a Lotus Elan – luckily, I'm a pro at the art of poppin' a clutch, since we have to push and pop, most of the time to get it running.

Well, back to Richard - he's an all-out wonderful guy. We fill something for one another, but I'm not sure what. For him, there was Jane. For me, Declan…yeah, just Declan, though, because I know Joe's a Lost Soul.

God, I want to be happy. I want peace, harmony, serenity – they are all distinctly different things, BTW.
OOPS…slipping into the approaching decades, again. That should read, 'by the way'. Memories…ya know?!
Wow…didn't realize the word 'peaceful' originated in the Middle East in about 1250: wonders never cease, huh?

Yes, peaceful can mean serene, but serenity is different than peacefulness in this case – serene, calm, tranquil – it's a feeling of, almost, extreme well being, but with no high emotion. It's all just quiet and calm. So, PEACE. PAX. PACE. PAIX. SALAM. SHALOM. FRIEDEN. TLALEGWA. WOWAHWA. Not so sure about that last one (Lakota, Sioux).

Well, anyhow, Richard and I decide to go out dancing one night and we head for the only (probably, the first) 'disco' in Bloomington. Who knows what was playing – okay, okay...it had a good beat and was easy to dance to.... what can I say that wasn't said, years before, on American Bandstand?! Heya Dick!

We're out on the dance floor, being cool and rhythmic, and dancing up a veritable storm, when I look around and spot this tall, dark-haired guy, wearing what looks like a white linen (?!) suit and moving around like a freakin' pro...A JOHN TRAVOLTA FREAKIN' PRO!

I dance over, with Dickie following, close. OMG! You guessed it – Declan! I should've known he could dance like that – after all, we sure did some pretty grand gymnastics, ourselves! He spots me just as I assume a look of complete horror.

MAN, NEXT TIME I'M STAYIN' ON THAT FREAKIN' SPACESHIP, I SWEAR, thinks I!

He arrives directly in front of me in just a couple strides: damn, those long legs of his. I spin around, grab Dickie, and hightail it not only off the dance floor, but out of the building, then make a run for the Lotus and holler back at Dickie to hurry up because I'm not feeling all that great.

I look back and Declan's following me, propelling his way through the tight group of dancing fools, packed on the hardwood floor.

I'm thrilled (well, not really) the Lotus starts and we don't have to jump it. I turn and Declan's just exited the building, staring at me, hands in his pockets and looking sad, as we screech away. I'm driving. I'm flying.

I never saw him again. Wonder if I ever *will* see him, ever again.
I hope he's not dead, because there's a part of me, I left back there, with him, May 30, 1971, and I'd hoped I'd be able to retrieve it someday. Always thought I'd have the time to return. Are we each other's missing pieces?
Wouldn't it be funny as all get out, if he never really thought of me at all?

I hate locked boxes, especially when I'm in them.

Donchu believe it…jokes on all of us….
BHH/PERSISTENT MEMORIES/MARCH 2016/BOCA GRANDE, FL

BLOMINGTON, IN/1974/PHYSICS/INTRO ASTRONOMY: Okay, so here I go, off to satisfy a curriculum (science) requirement. Professor L. Pataki, teacher.

I was told, when I was about eight years old, that girls don't really need to know math and why in the heck did I ever believe that one?

I get to class and the prof is very animated and interesting. He announces that if anyone needs extra help, to stay after

76

on Mondays and Wednesdays and we'll have a study session, so, I do.

I LOVE this teacher – he's freaking awesome! This guy makes math and science fun and if I'd had him as a teacher in grade school, or even in high school, I'd probably be a freakin' astrophysicist, instead of a prelaw major, majoring in sociology (I DO love my mentor, F. W., though) and political science. EFP...

So, Dr. Pataki has just shown us how to figure a Doppler shift and I can actually compute one, now hmmm...wonder if Mom and Dad would be upset if I added physics to my major's list?

But everything that I genuinely believe can pretty well be disproved by math and physics, well, anyway what we know, thus far, and I guess that's my point and my hope is – that the things I know (intuitively) are true, will one day, be proven (mathematically/scientifically).

I'm talking past lives, here, and time travel and astral projection. "One Day, Raju, but not today".
BHH/JOURNALED ON THE BACK OF AN OLD COPY OF *LITTLE BUDDHA* SCRIPT/1993

COTE D'IVOIRE/1977: Sick. God help me, I'm so sick I might just die. Been coming out both ends, and I can't figure out how in the heck I got malaria, since I took all those damned pills for weeks before I got here.

Man, it's been one thing after another.

First, I arrive in Lagos, and I'm kept at the airport for hours, until I agree to pay a bribe. Then, I'm attacked by biting

77

ants while I'm asleep and *then* become deathly ill and doc says I have malaria.

Oba takes us in for questioning and insists on putting us up in the Holiday Inn on Victoria Island – we know we're being watched and very carefully, because Liz's mom got out of prison right before we arrived (she's from a very important and very a political family). That's what I remember, anyway; and hell, who knows if it's true or if it's my brain's way of buffaloing me and my memories.

By the time they tell me a chief has died and they're eyeing me for the accompanying burial; I've had enough and I'm ready to fly to the Ivory Coast, if the General and S. will let me come early – if only we could reach them, by phone. Remember, it's 1977 and cell phones weren't even a glimmer.

I'm so sick I don't know what's real and what's not and I'm getting sicker by the day, it seems.

I've had a deep, deep desire to travel to Africa since I was a kid and now, here I am, and I just might DIE here. Not the first time and won't be the last, for this Old Soul.
BHH/JOURNAL AFRIQUE
JOURNAL/1998/TILGHMAN ISLAND, MD

2015/CABIN/NC BLUE RIDGE MTS/BARB'S STUDIO: Going through boxes and boxes and boxes of crap that Jack and I have toted around, stored, filed away, stashed etc., etc.

Lo and behold, what do I find? My diaries from when Jack and I first moved in together/my letters to him and his to me. OMG! What was I thinking?! Better yet: <u>was</u> I thinking? With which part of my body? Yeah, you got it.

Cut myself some slack, because by then, I was already swimming in the love. Yeppers, Red Ryder, I believe I was (in love), and probably pretty deep drowning, hit by that good ole emotional tsunami. Shit, I'm struggling between the spirit and the organic all the time. Guess which usually wins?

I must have realized, early on in this life, I was meant to be Jack's support and try my best to be a decent example and hold him up. He told me, right before he died, that he couldn't have been or done what he was/did without me. I already knew that, but I was sure happy to hear he knew it, too. It was always the elephant in our room and I am immensely grateful he verbalized it.

He says, Barb, you gave up your dreams for me: so, if I go first, you promise me you'll finish the books and write and travel and walk the ancient Ire sites and crawl around Mount Rushmore and be a stupid tourist. Be happy. Find.... Well...find Love...you know...

Yes, says I. Jack and I had no secrets - he knew all about Declan.

Now, I am, writing at least. This occurred to me, last night, but has run through my brain, many times, before - when Jack got on one knee (he really, really did) and proposed...he says:

Babe, if you want a picket fence that ain't gonna happen, with me.
But, I'll take you on one hell of a Magical Mystery Tour and We'll have one <u>hell</u> of a lot of fun.
We'll never be rich, but,
We will be *rich,* and
We'll be artists and

We'll make cool shit and
We'll fuckin' fight and
We'll fuckin' make up and
We'll do all kinds of crazy, wonderful things...and,
if we throw our lots in, together....I promise….
You'll never be bored.

It didn't.
He did.
We did.
We weren't.
We were/are.
We were/are.
We did.
We did.
We did.
We did.
We did.
I wasn't.

RECAP: Barb, if you want a picket fence that ain't gonna
happen, with me - **IT DIDN'T**
(Then, says I...you're kidding, right?! Really? Me? -
Picket fence?! Yeah, *right*....)
But, I'll take you on one hell of a Magical Mystery Tour -
HE DID and
(Then, says I… years later, WOW...*Will You Still Love*
***Me*?) (EGADS! I <u>AM</u> 64!)**
We'll have one hell of a lot of fun - **WE DID**
(Then, says I...Uhhh...exactly, how do <u>you</u> define
***fun*?)**
We'll never be rich - **WE WEREN'T** but,
(Then, says I...are we <u>still</u>
completely/unreservedly/totally broke?)
We'll be *rich* – **WE WERE/ARE** and
(Then, says I...Now I know the 'why'…)

80

We'll be artists - **WE WERE/ARE** and
(Then, says I: You fuckin' amaze me, Jack...)
We'll make cool shit - **WE DID** and
(**Then, says I...I'm all for cool, yeah, we ARE
cool...but let's make some moola, too!**)
We'll fuckin' fight - **WE DID** and
(**Then, says I: Bubba, you're right, there ARE two
Alpha Males in this marriage!**)
We'll fuckin' make up - **WE DID** and
(**Then, says I...C'mon.... let's just leave it alone and go
back to the fuckin' part....k?**)
We'll do all kinds of crazy, wonderful things - **WE
DID**...and,
(**Then, says I - Geez, didn't really know you meant
certifiable.....**)
If we throw our lots in, together - **WE DID**....
(**Then, says I...uh, as in _married_?!**) I promise.... you'll
never be bored, Barb, and I mean NEVER... **I WASN'T -
EVER** (**Then, says I.... You made good that most
important promise, Darlin' Jack.... Thank you. I love
you to the last number.**)
TRUTH: When Scooter was four, he says to me: Mommy,
I love you to the Last Number, and I say There is no last
number, Sweet Pea.
He pulled me close and whispers, Mommy, my Love goes
on and on. It _never_ ends!

Fuckin'a...C what I mean? Spaceship's barreling right at
me....beam me up, Alice...er...Scottie!
BHH/DREAMING/IRE/PARIS/ISTANBUL
MARRAKECH/KATHMANDU????
GOODFRIDAY/2016/MEA CULPA

2025/COLORADO: Here's the thing, NT - I have to write
through the pain. Write through the sorrow, through the
joy, through the fear, the anger, the hurt, all the crazy

81

memories, regardless of what they were and how joyful, or painful, or frightening they were. Because all these lives intertwine so beautifully, you'd think I'm creating the most intricate, awesome illuminated manuscript that's ever been conceived. In many ways I am. So are you and don't you forget it.

The journey, regardless of what we'd all like to believe is a solitary one and I'm out on this trail, completely alone, because Pathfinder's dead and NT's nowhere to be found, but I suspect he just headed home…but I'm not alone – not really. And, neither are you. We're, none of us, genuinely alone.

I remember when we picked up Jack (living above that deli in downtown Annapolis) to take him to yet another rehab, after I asked him to gather his things and just leave, when I found that huge bottle of pills and him, supposedly straight and sober. Yeah, yeah, I never <u>blamed</u> him…his cells cried out for sustenance and he fed them. Genes…But my sponsor did tell me this would become a pattern if I didn't, you know, nip it in the bud. OMG it practically killed me…mostly because I'd known Jack (Pathfinder) as a stalwart warrior and my best friend, many times; so, to see him in these compromised circumstances was painful, to say the least. He constantly battled his enemy, in this life, but it was substances, instead of people. He always swore it was people.

You know, many lives ago, because he was six feet tall and enormously powerful, it was nothing to kill his enemies and mine – he was always my protector. Harder, this time. Damn near impossible. You can flush 'em, you can throw 'em away, you can burn 'em, but you can't kill booze and drugs and they're always available. I figured it was a losing battle, but, in the end, love won out and I stayed…it's always a victory when love wins out, because everything, it seems, wants to turn it, shift it away, undermine it. That's a dangerous statement on many levels, NT, and especially having you read it. The saving grace is that love doesn't always need to be 24/7. Love is love and that's saying something.

If Jack had been a normal guy, and by that, I mean not an addict/alcoholic or obsessive/compulsive or a freaking genius – if he'd just been your run-of-the-mill genius or even a drone, I might have played my cards differently – I might've *played* or left.

You know, had the stones to 'not care' as much and skipped down some of those other paths that presented themselves at various junctures on my road but, he was that addict, alcoholic, compulsive, genius and so I didn't. I stayed. I Loved him.

As it should be, for the time we were together.
He counted on me and I (disliking promises, not kept, as I do) stood firm.

Yes, there were times I thought I might waiver and leave, but had I – well, I knew Jack would not last if I did, because I knew Jack so passionately, so completely: his vulncrabilities, as well as every bright facet he possessed.

Jack simply could not take a breath that did not fill my lungs. Period.

For a time, we shared every part of who we are and were; but now I let him go.

It's just the way of things. Every time. I'm not complaining. It was time for him to leave. I have a journey to complete and I'm anxious to get going, back into it.

In the end, who can be counted upon? You. Yourself; alone. That's it. It's a lonely road, but even if you don't want to walk it, you do. You have to. You can sit in a chair your entire freakin' life playing vids and never, ever move - but in the end, **that** will be the road, the path, the journey you were supposed to walk. The one you chose, before you arrived here, in this time and place.

Me? I write through all of it. Right now, I'm walking and writing deliberate.

It doesn't matter who's found and who remains lost – or, hidden. Not really. We find who we need to find, and we find them when we can each do one another the most good – even if it seems like the most harm. The Universe or God or Bubba – whatever you choose to label it, has some plan, I guess. Unrevealed, to us, mere humans…but with God, somewhere inside, right?

That's my story and I'm walking and writing through it….

I know I'll find Declan if and when I'm supposed to - heck, we located one another once, already, so half the intent is over. Now it's just working the remainder.

I have a hole in my chest where my heart used to be and it needs filling… let's see where this road leads. It's all good. Well, even if it isn't all good (in my eyes) it really is and sometimes I can't see all those dots to connect them and I sure as hell can't see the entire picture.

84

Tomorrow, I head out and hope I catch up with…someone. Never did relish traveling alone, but I've done it most of my lives. I have lots of time…. time to think…. time to look ahead and back, unfortunately.

But I do see how all the tiny moments echo and warp and fit so snugly into one another and it's all so subtle that we don't, generally, even notice all the nuances. Sometimes it blows me away and I find myself thinking *What else have I missed?* I can't dwell, not for one second, on what I <u>didn't</u> do - there's much that's Kafkaesque about the shit I DID do, the decisions I DID make: this looking back is terrible/wonderful and there are flashes when my synapses recall what someone said or how someone reached for me - and I turned away.

Ergo, everything is perfect - it <u>must</u> be - if it were not, then none of us would possess any surety and none of us could possibly be confident about this life, this particular life, we lead.

Maybe it was different when we were all warriors and living by our prowess and our wits. We must've had our hand on a sword every second of every day. Yeah, we did and I'm grateful to be out of *that*, but there's no guarantee these existences are <u>linear</u>.

Humans invented time and so, what we think we know, may not, in the universe's reality, actually BE true. It's all relative and I believe Albert would agree.

In the end, I do wonder if I'll have to return to that brutal way of life, then, I think, this one has its own kind of brutality:

There you are. Here I am.

These are difficult days for me, right now. I do have faith - faith there is purpose and intent in all our moments, in everything each of us shares with one another; but today a sadness wants to permeate my thoughts and settle in and pull me down and I'm a scrapper from way back, so I can't allow it - can't let it win. Hope it does not win.

I guess, in the end, stars or stones - doesn't really matter because they are the same: same energy, just different vehicle. That's what I must remember when the organic attempts to overcome the spirit - my spirit.

I think I should be writing this into my story. Writing to YOU really does inspire me to think harder, longer, more completely about all this stuff. I wonder why you have that affect upon me...it doesn't matter, because you do.
I love you. That's what matters. Love.
BHH/ON VELLUM, DATED 2030/COLORADO TRAIL AFTER THE DEVASTATION

1833/DUSK/BLUE RIDGE MOUNTAINS: Always did say a kiss is just about as intimate as you can get – exchanging breath and sharing breath, which feeds our 'organic parts' with oxygen, is pretty personal.

I first saw Pathfinder out of the corner of my eye – he was crouched among the bushes, arrow nocked, drawn and ready, watching a white tail deer. Someday Jack and I, in another life, will purchase an early map, which labels all the lands west of the Mississippi as "Parts Unknown". But on that early autumn day in those thick woods, when I was (then) seventeen well, it was I, who was in parts unknown: first time love.)

86

I moved only an inch, but it was far enough to snap the twig and cause the deer to leap up and away. Pathfinder stood, his arm and arrow dropped to his side and the arrow slid from the bow, dead on the ground.

That stare…

Yes, I stared at her, says Pathfinder. She was a yellow hair, but she wore Iroquois clothes. She crouched and stared back.

Her skin was so white – washed in moonbeams. I had to walk toward her, to see if she was real.

She drew me to her; like some magic force was calling and I couldn't turn away.

I stood directly in front of her and reached for her to take my hand. She did…I helped her up and we just stood there, gawking at each other.

Finally says I, who are you?
Raven's Moon, says she.

She cupped her hand at the base of my skull and pulled me to her lips.

Never look back.

1983/ANNAPOLIS, MD: I found one of the loves of my many lives, today, Mama. I don't know his name, but I know I'm gonna marry him.
BHH/FROM A DREAM/WAKEFULNESS STATE
JACK AND I SHARED - DIARY

Reversal

by Barbara Helvey Hughes
For Chris Hughes, Declan Niall, & Mason

Life unravels eternal
Like the strands of a braided rope.
A bundle of individual, twisted strings
All hangin' akimbo, yet each reality
Bound as one and a million intersecting
Events – all connected and growing
On top of each other, like tumors
Eating us away from the inside, out.
Disentangled, a strand whips away.
Another snaps! One frays –
Where are you?
The Dream ambushes me, spirals down.
Down, down the vortex, spinnin' characters
I know I know, but who appear/disappear
In and out, like taunting shadows tryin' to be real.
Someone looked at me today. Eye bored
Right to my Core. Uneasy, I slipped away
Then thought 'I know him.' but never met him.
Not in this life. That electrical
Charge runnin' down my spine, arm hairs
Upright, a jolt from the past. Or future?
Where are you?
You are somewhere. Jus' not here.
Meanin', not here, in front of me.
Can't see you with eyes, but see you.
I'd know that n-ergy anywhere.
You're out there. But if I spend all my
Time lookin' fer you, I wōn live this Life.
Gotta let go. Move forward. Forget.
Easy said. Hard done.
You comin' at me?

When? You lookin' too?
Cain't find what wōn be found. Lost.
Drum up that Beacon, Baby.
Dark ways leave me turn'd 'roun'.
Gone. Gone. Gone.
Forgivin' the loss – at's the hardess thin'.
Clip 'at wōn frum memry.
I cain't do dis 'lone.
You here?

Hurd da whispr last eve. Like a
Bug in ma ear hummin', hummin'
Hummin' 'way – givin' me an
Eye fulla fall/down vert-i-go. It diggin' deep.
Niv'r u min', Heartbeat.
Niv'r u giv it 'nother fleet thought.
U ain't here. I am. My probl'm.
You close?

Days move thru me like jolt/bolt lightnin'.
Decks all shuffled, mixed-up confused.
Cain't recall feelin' so discombobulated.
One string crossin' over 'nother.
All tangle into non-sense.
Dis-ease means I ain't at ease.
Ping! 'Nother one snap loose.
Wind flutt'r. Mind bomb. Heart 'splode.
Layin' down. Cain't rise. You help?

You tol' me Love.
Jus' a werd.
I goin' back.
Back ta stardus' what made me.
Thots a'jumbl a'nuthin'.
Slinkin' bak ta toddl-hood
Afor' I go.

Niv'r did finja.
Shuda stop lukin' lon-go.

I nivr wanna c u 'gin.
Fallin' lo. Rōpz war-out.
Nun strings lef'.
Lōnsum an' lōn.
U not hear. I here. Not long.

We bak here ta do sumthin'.
I dun do nuthin'. 'Cept luk fer u.
My hart brokin', Heartbeat.
I cumon bak, wōn day?
Dunno.

It is said, there are no do-overs
With this precious Lifegift;
Evenso, here I walk, again, on this
Circle of Light. Back here, with
Brain-firing synapses, trying to
Set those memories right and
Figure it out. The view is very
Confusing, from this crib, where I rest.
I can't talk. Yet. But; I know.
I am born, knowing. So are you.
More than likely, we're at our finest,
Our most intuitive selves, when we can't
Utter a word, but can only stare at the
Space where the wall and ceiling meet.
What do we see there? Angles? Angels?

One tentative step leads to another.
Pretty soon, the reality we find
Ourselves flung into, is the only
One we see. But echoes whisper
From before. From some other place.

Another time.
Shadows tumble around us.
They hide. We seek.

In this crib, all snug as a bug,
I remember it all. I want to
Tell you. It burns my mouth,
How badly I want to speak.
My brain and throat don't work
Together, at this early stage.
And - I'm scared of forgetting.

So, I gaze at you, Mom,
And try to talk to you with my eyes.
You can't hear me. Too busy with
Making sure I'm safe, to hear the
Whisperspeak. It's okay.
By the time I can talk, those
Shadow stories, from before,
Will be all but gone – they will have left me.
Mostly.
And I'll begin again.
But if I do say something and a shiver spins up
Your spine, then listen and think!
I might just be telling you a Secret.

I Love you.

1997/TILGHMAN ISLAND, MD/EARLY MORNING:
and I just arose...Jack's not in bed and panic grips my heart.
Where is he? I run downstairs and search the first floor, but
he's not there. I enter the kitchen and look out the big
window, toward the foggy shore – there he is, with his head
against the old locust tree, the one lightning struck, the one
he's concerned about – the one where someone could get
hurt. That hundred-year-old tree.

Jack stands in front of Tree and leans into her. His forehead rests against her and because I know that's the way Jack sometimes communicates, I figure he and Tree are talking or performing some kind of energy/info exchange. I make coffee and head out for my studio.

I enter my studio and begin my prayers and meditations, occasionally glancing out the French doors at Jack, still positioned at Tree like a statue. An hour later, I'm done. Weekends at home are such a gift, because I can actually meditate and feel as if I've been engaged in the process, instead of rushing through it, checking the time and knowing I can't get Scoot to school, late. But most weekends, we travel to a show. It's a hectic life…no time to breathe…

I start a new necklace design and play with several colors, deciding upon shades of greens and purples. No one, to my knowledge, has done these colours, so it will be something new and exciting to present in NYC, next month. We exhibit three consecutive weekends, twice a year, at the Columbus Avenue Craft Fair – we are known as *Bright Bear* and our booth has been anchored on the corner of 81st and Columbus Avenue for many, many years. We've developed quite a following in The City. Jack and I fabricate all our own designs, and, with the exception of a few components, we make most of our jewelry the week before each show. People expect new and exciting art wearables from us, and we try not to disappoint; but there's Jack still standing like a pillar of salt at Tree. It's been a couple hours, now, and I wonder if he's all right or has he accidentally glued his tongue to Tree. (double dog dare ya!)

The fog has become like soup, and I can barely see Jack, as I descend the studio steps and walk toward him. I gently place my hand on his right shoulder - Are you okay, Sweetheart?

He stirs and pulls away from Tree, smiles vaguely and says, I'm okay - I just have to stay here with her and make her understand…don't be concerned – I'll probably be here most of the day. I start back to my studio as Scooter arrives in my open arms: Mom, says he, is Dad okay, what's he doin'? He's okay, says I, he's just talking with Tree.

Later that day, as I prepare supper and watch Jack, still poised against Tree, I wonder if he's fallen asleep or if he and Tree are still conversing: I get my answer, almost as soon as the thought skips through my brain. Jack steps away from her and places a hand on her trunk, for a second, then turns and walks to the house. He's had no breakfast or lunch and he must be famished. The roast is almost done, but Jack enters and says I gotta lay down – that took a lot outta me. He heads up the stairs.

Later, Jack descends the stairs and sits at the kitchen table, which has always been the center of this 1880's home.
Wanna talk? says I.
I'm takin' her down, says he, already talked with Kevin and he's bringing the truck tomorrow. She's far-gone and she's got so much dead wood that if the kids start climbing her again, they will get hurt.
Sure she's dead? says I.
Yep, says Jack, and I'm starving…smells great.

Next day Jack and Kevin are at it early. They've positioned a chain around Tree and as Kevin puts it in gear, the truck lurches, but doesn't move far. I watch Pathfinder (Jack) scratch his head and talk with Kev. Jack retrieves the chainsaw, and Kevin pulls his out of the truck bed – they whine as the cut begins. I know Jack wanted to avoid any possible "blood"-letting. Lucky the sap has had its run down Tree's trunk.

Abruptly: silence. In my studio, I rise and go to the doors, look out, just as Kevin unhooks the chain, tosses it into the truck and gently pulls away – while Jack, looking distraught, leans his back into Tree and slides down to sit at her base. I know better than to go to him…this is serious, and I understand what's going on, so I must wait.

Jack has taught me patience in this life – the hard way.

Tears well in my eyes and I can't watch any more. Chris has been out on Devil's Island, the island just offshore, where Captain John B. Harrison (who built our house) built his famous log canoes. DI is but a memory of what it once was, because the currents and tides have taken their heavy toll, but during low tide you can still have a great time finding all kinds of treasure and that's what Chris and his friends often do – like today. I see him jump in his jonboat and head towards shore. He ties it up and walks down the lane to our home, spots Jack and startles. He stops, tentatively: I've stepped out to my studio porch and wave him up. He tiptoes past Jack and takes the stairs two at a time.

Mom, says he, is Dad okay? I think something's wrong! We'll find out tonight, Sweetie, says I. Let him be, for now. Let's go in and I'll make you some lunch.

Later that evening, Jack finally stood and, again, placed his hand on Tree's trunk then came inside. As he entered, I could see he was upset.
I took him in my arms, and he just whispered, She's not dead, Babe. I made a big mistake, so I've been telling her I planted her seeds all over the property. I think she'll be okay, now.

I held Pathfinder at arms-length and quickly, my mind raced back over the past spring and summer as I watched him tenderly uproot and move dozens of saplings, which he carefully mowed around and planted in the most beneficial places.

That's what you were doing, whispers I.

In that moment, I understood Love on an entirely new level – mine for him and his for all creatures: especially the ones who couldn't talk back...
This is a true story. For sure.
I couldn't make this shit up if I tried.

I told her she will prevail, and her children will populate this land for generations to come, Babe, says he, I think she's okay - she should release and come down more easily, tomorrow.

She did.

We were the owners of that property long enough to see the fruits of Jack's labours. In springtime, down by the water where Jack and Scooter had their hammock and loved to swing and listen to the lapping of the water, the air was always laced with the heady, sweet, thick fragrance of the locust blossoms – can't get much more beautiful a smell than that.
Can't have a much better memory than that...
BHH/BOCA GRANDE, FL/AFTER JACK – MARCH 2016/8 MONTHS, TODAY

974/IRE: They keep coming at us, U'Neill and his tribe. Do they, truly, have no fear or are they simply stupid? I've been afraid all my life – thrown into this position when my father

died and all I've known all these years, has been the tinny taste of fear in my mouth. Fear crawling up my spine. Fear gripping my gut as I ride into battle. I am sick to death of fear and fear will be the death of me.
BHH/DREAM/1994/MATHGHAMHAIN/NIAMH MAHON/BEAR/BRIGHTBEAR

PLACIDA, FL/2016/MARCH 30: I arose, early, and started my daily edit on *EFP*. Reading back, I see clearly just how easy it is to succumb to the fear. Are we plagued with it through all our lives, or is it more prevalent in some, than in others?

I guess my big fear, this time, would have to be Jack. Would he make it or would he give in and give up? Through sickness and through health/till death do us part – right on, Red Ryder. Mission Accomplished. Challenge lifted, shifted, gone, and Pathfinder found his Path and (well, pretty much, anyhow) walked it. He *became* and that's all he ever asked to do. How beautiful. And he assisted me, incredibly, in my 'becoming journey', but I'm still walking and I can't wait to see what unfolds next.

I'll be sixty-five years old in exactly two months. I'm done with fear. When I released Jack/Pathfinder/Niamh, I released fear. I no longer partner with what ifs or shouldas/couldas/wouldas. Nada has no place in the remainder of my current life and I do my best to live in the now and not project anything; not project fear, especially. I've always believed life is a gift and I've done my due diligence, this time, in most all respects – have carried out the orders with the freakin' precision of a surgeon and have stayed the course – battle fought and won. That's how I choose to see it, anyhow.

96

I'm not searching for another soul or spirit, because I know if they're supposed to find me, they will. I can 'call the Ancient Ones' to me, all I like, but my "voice" only travels so far… if they're not invested, then they can get a freaking hearing aid and don't blame me if we never re-connect and finish our chapters.

Of course, you know the only one I can't let go…. Jack is Dead/NT, alive & found me/Declan? Don't know, but thinking he might just be in California/JFC is dead - California Dreamin'? Ain't nuthin' keeping me here.

Just remembering the other eve about Declan and me…. we ended up at a local baseball game and he led me way up high to the top bleachers. He sat and I stood in front of him, with his arms wrapped around me. He kept leaning into my hair and smelling me. I loved it when he did that. I keep thinking to myself about how deeply I felt for him, and I pretty much knew he was Thee One and I LOVED him somethin' terrible. Then, he buried his face in my hair and angled over to my ear and whispered, I Love you so much. I thought I'd faint, but thought better of it, whirled around to face him and got real close – you know how when your lips are so close they might melt together if you move a nano-inch? That close. Might be obscenely close to some…I said, I love you so much, too. And I turned back around, and he wound his arms around me again, and pulled me even closer. I got skin in this game, Baby.

Can you hear me, Declan? Did you know that a deep and intense rivalry existed between your ancient forebears and mine? Yours, in Northern Ire and mine, in the South…. long before Romeo and Juliet ever dreamed of entering that life, in Italy. Of course – that would be the way of things, eh? Maybe that's why we've had such a hard time this time, you know, connecting. Maybe not. Maybe shit just happens

and there's no 'reason'. Don't know. Let's find one another and obliterate all that thousand-year-old crap...Love conquers all, or so they say.
BHH/DRAGGIN' MY FEET TOWARD MARIN COUNTY/HEADING FOR MY FAV/SAM'S/TIBURON/ WRITTEN ON PALACE HOTEL STATIONERY/DATED,1981/SF, CA/FOUND, MARCH 30, 2016

2008/OCTOBER/OUT HOME – INDIANA FARM:
Mom's been in and out of the hospital for a couple months, now. I know this will be my last stretch of time with her, in this life, and I'm ever so grateful she lived so long. Mom and I sort of grew up together, this time – she became my friend when I went to college and she's become my dearest friend, my champion, my teacher, my mentor, my confidant. The least I can do for her is to be here as she winds down and winds homeward; so, I stay for months and sometimes we just sit.

Jack's the one who alerted me to the congestive heart failure facet and that wouldn't have happened if her Lafayette doc hadn't insisted upon giving her pharmaceuticals for osteoporosis, after he screwed up her replaced hip. What a nasty bugger he was – I took Mom in, because one leg was much longer than the other and when he examined her and yanked on her leg I almost decked him – I would've if Mom hadn't been there, but if she hadn't been there, I wouldn't have been there, either.

That clinic reminded me of a slaughterhouse – just herdin' 'em in, Ma'am…. don't blame me, I didn't make the rules…yeah, that's what they all say, right? Just following orders…how do these assholes ever even become doctors?! There should be a panel to review how they treat their fellow humans – every one of them, but I know some really compassionate and kind, loving ones, too – just not <u>that</u> one.

But she was ready to go, or at least that's what Bubba says. She never told me that - she knew I couldn't take it. I was a big ole baby when it came to Mom and it took me almost a year and a half not to cry when someone mentioned her. Couple years not to tear up. Now, I can talk about her, most times, and not cry. Anyhow, whoever says shame on you when it's hard to let someone you love go, well, you know what I say, right? I say fuck 'em if they can't take a joke.
BHH/JUST FINISHED *NO TRACE, CLYMERS*/2013/EDIT/AFTER MOM/NOTEBOOK NUMBER 2

SANFRAN/CA/APRIL 30, 1906: Lucky to be alive after the quake on April 18th. Lost everything and happy I didn't lose my life – many did. Had hoped to be outta San Fran by the 18th, but of course the quake struck in the early morning hours and chaos ensued. Grabbed what I could and made my way outta the firetrap – everything was ablaze. Headed toward the bay in hopes of making my way out of the city, maybe by boat, but death and mayhem were everywhere, and no one had the forethought or wherewithal to make a plan. Even Caruso, who had sung at the Grand Opera House, (I saw him perform) had a hard time escaping that city and he vowed never to return – not great press for an already devastated place. The Palace Hotel came down like a house made of sticks and the fires were downright frightening. Caruso was staying there, too.

I decided to stay on and help as much as I could. I'd give my eyeteeth to hook back up with NT or Declan: but they might one, or both, be gone to their heavenly (well, maybe not…) rewards. …. Where R U Declan?

I'm sweeping and cooking and whatever they need me to do, before I set out on my road. Might take the riverboat back…always did want to follow these rivers – see where they go. Lots of women never do have these opportunities and I figure I'd best grab onto them, if I can (without harm to my person, that is).

Maybe, in some lives, we are more fragile than in others…do we retain personality characteristics from life to life? Who knows…but, I do think we must keep certain tendencies - my warrior bend comes out in most situations, and I've spent my entire life pretty much fighting for the underdog or the ones who can't fight for themselves…. a lot of men can't handle it and, instead of partnering with me, they become combative. It's a rara avis, who can handle a strong woman. Of course, Declan could. (well – maybe?) Jack could (sometimes) (not very well) (ok, ok….he really didn't), NT could.

Typhoid outbreak. Fingers crossed and I'm hightailing it out of here!
BHH/SWING LOW SWEET CHARIOT AND TAKE ME HOME/NO PALACE HOTEL STATIONERY LEFT NOW/JUST PAPERS BUNCHED TOGETHER/1906/GOING HOME/ WHERE BE THAT?

APRIL 1, 2016/ YEAH, GET THIS, APRIL FOOL'S DAY/CAN'T BELIEVE IT/PINCH ME:
After years of searching for Declan – dare I say half-hearted? Was I afraid I might actually <u>find</u> him and so, did not put on the most thorough search, because of Pathfinder? Yes: totally true. I can't even go back there, because I have way too much skin in that particular game. Too much soul, too.

Yep, I paid the $99 to get access to all those files they have on-line and I put in everything I knew about him and all the variants and I found him. Then confirmed it on email.

For the first time in forty-five years or more I am talking to the one I would have died for, the one I have always Loved more than my life, the Love _of_ my life. I heard his email voice, too – oh, Mercy….
BHH/FREAKIN OUT/FREAKIN'A

APRIL 6, 2016/EMOTION'S MOTION/SPINNING SPOKES
I have talked with Declan Sunday, Monday, and tonight, Wednesday…
I'm gathering stars.
BHH/FLYIN' 'ROUND JUPITER

APRIL/2016: Can't sleep and can't wait for us to meet again, in this life. Thrilled that this has come about and how it did: I was picking up the pieces of my glass heart from all over the floor at the gallery and I was crying. Something burrowing deep into my soul, hooked in and wouldn't release me. Declan's been on my mind since the day Jack passed. That's a lie…he's been on my mind and in my heart since May 30, 1971…my twentieth birthday. On March 30, 2016, I sat at my gallery computer, looked up and said, Jack, you know how I Loved Declan. Please guide me back to him. Couple days later and I'd found him…. thank you, Dear One.

OMG…he's divorced and no ties…are some relationships written in the stars? Jack needed me and I stayed. I knew Dec could make good on his own and back then we had very different goals. God, I've missed the _feel_ of him, his smell, his energy, his Love…. can it be possible? Declan

101

simply couldn't have a thought that didn't enter my soul.
Let us find our ways home to one another before it's too
late.
Is it too late?
2016/AFTER JACK DIARY #1

1971/SUMMER/DC: Before I left IU, Declan asked me to
go with him, to Maroc.... I wanted to go, with all my heart,
but I knew I couldn't...my path didn't include the games he
was playing at that stage: high stakes games. And there was
trouble brewing on all fronts. He was really upset with me
and although we kissed and held close, as we parted, I knew
– I felt his energy and it was pissed and confused and
hurt....and, me, not wanting to piss him off, hurt or
confuse him – me, just wanting to jump back into his arms,
but I simply couldn't....I had a vision from long, long ago
and here I was standing at the fork in my path – you know,
the really big fork. Yeah, it's the *'fuckin'a, you gotta make a
choice here, Girly, Girl and ain't nobody gonna take yer hand an' help
ya out – you must choose. Choose wisely'.*

How the heck can ya choose wisely, when you're only
twenty years old? In the end – did I choose wisely? That's
the $64,000 question – I guess I did because I lived this life
and everything's perfect, right? Yeah...*right.*

Declan left, and I drove to DC...there's a lot more to the
story, but right now my skin's pretty thin thinking about it,
so let me just tell you what happened, later, that summer.
Declan arrived in DC. Heading to Maroc. We made love
and I was on cloud nine, but he was distant and still upset
with me. We drove to a park and hung out. He kept asking
me to go with him and he was more persistent.... I didn't
even have a passport, so there was no way. He said I could
get one and he'd wait, change his flight...Christ, why is life
so hard?

Finally, when I did drive him to the airport and we said goodbye, we stood there hugging and I was crying my eyes out. He hid his face in my hair and I thought he might've been crying, too…then he whispered: Just remember, Barbara, you left me first.

He kissed me again and started away. Our arms were entwined, and I remember thinking how they were like two threads of a once strong rope, unwinding, unraveling, pulling apart (I wrote that poem *Reversal* inspired by this event, by Declan and by my son and grandson - because I know *it's all true*) until, finally, our arms were no longer touching, we had unspun and my heart had been ripped off its tether and it thumped to the ground, still pumping. Blood all over. I stared at my organic heart on those antiseptic white tiles, through an ocean of tears and, to my horror, I gaped at the scene as though it were a movie and the evil culprit was finally revealed – aghast, I saw the villain – it was me.

Declan didn't allow my poor heart to bleed out too long, before he tenderly reached down, picked it up and cradled it, in his arms, blood dripping across the terminal floor. He walked away. Yeah, he did look back. How can I ever forget that look? When I see you next my Dearest One, let there be light in your eyes. Let me see you, again - why are we always walking away?

'Just remember, Barbara, you left me first' – yes, I do remember, and I have remembered for more than forty years…it's tattooed on my heart, and I just might have it tattooed across my freakin' chest to remind me what a stoopid idiot I was; but, Baby, no regrets, not really.

There you are, Honey. Here I am.

APRIL 7, 2016/EARLY MORNING LOVER/GOING
DOWN/DOWN BELOW THE FLOOR

1980/SANFRAN/PALACE HOTEL/WH
FREEMAN/SCIENTIFIC AMERICAN/PUBLISHER:
How can this possibly be? I know this place. Walking
through the doors, greeted by the Bellman, I startle. There's
a message. Strawberries and cream under the dome?
2016 WRITTEN IN A RANDOM NOTEBOOK OF
POETRY FROM 1981/AM I ALWAYS FOUND?

JAN. 1971/SOPHOMORE BLUES/INDIANA
UNIVERSITY/BLOOMINGTON: I have a feeling I'm
gonna be stuck in a time warp...I haven't met the energy
that keeps wrapping itself around me, but I sure do feel it.
Feels good, all snuggly and warm, but it scares me. I might
get lost, lose my way, and not live my intentions and that
frightens me...fear...God, how I hate it.

I remember riding that stallion into battle and my men all
battle-ready and furious, but I could feel the undercurrent
of fear; just... like... now.

Where the hell did that come from??!! I guess it don't matter
where it is, what life it was in, you can't forget it....it trails
behind you and you think wow, why am I recalling
something I never saw nor read; but your spirit knows –
you did see it. Just don't recall, because if we could recall all
those other spirits and times and places we just might not
possess the heart to live this one...but wherever this energy
is, I hope it finds me soon.

You see that spaceship angling over the woods, last night?

I'm pulling out my sword and staying at the ready, just in
case I'm ambushed, by that other, more aggressive

energy...Joe? Chief thinks I'm crazy, but he don't know the half of it. I don't recognize the entire piece to this part of my puzzle, either, but I got an inkling. Time, again, for a Heartbreak, Hartbreak? That ole stag goin' down, and I can already feel his hot breath on my neck. Damn, ain't no way I can eat that heart/hart. I just love him too damn much.... I know you're out there, somewhere; but *where* is the big question, huh?

Thirty miles away as the crow flies and I don't even know that, yet. That's to come...

So many energies coming at me, tugging me, wanting to know me. Lost. That's how I'm feeling. Rudderless. I gotta find that anchor...you know, the one who came back this time to find <u>me</u>...the One I need to find and love and stay with...but which one is it? Someone I haven't even met yet, in this life?!

What happens if I can't find him? Is that what hell is? Not finding your missing piece, the one who completes you, the one you made a sacred vow to find, before ya'll returned? What happens if you can't join back? When you pass along, do you have only half a soul? Half yourself?? Fuckin'a, man, I swear it's always something. I gotta get my shit together, put my back into it and study my ass off. BH/NO HUGHES YET/FOUND IN POETRY NOTEBOOK DATED 1972

1835/BLUE RIDGE MOUNTAINS: Built us a camp and the living is easy. Well, during most of the year. Pathfinder's family accompanied us, and we hardly had a moment alone. Yeah, well, we're the "Injuns" in the "uprising" I guess...Me and he will always be some kinda warriors and have some kinda love. Not sure what kind,

105

but some kind...ala John Stewart. But that's Declan's song. Or, is it?

I look out across the round top mountains, and I hear the ancient voices calling. Pathfinder didn't need to kidnap me, I went free and on my own, this time. He's gonna need my help again. Maybe it's only one life in a dozen or so, when we repeat those patterns. Let's hope.
BHH/DREAMWEAVING JOURNAL/2001

2015/PLACIDA, FL/WATCHING AND WAITING: I've been watching this JJ Abrams series, called *Lost*. Never could watch it on TV, because I didn't see the first of it and I have to see the first or I'm, well, *LOST*. Jack just passed away and all I can think is: should I try to pick up the trail of the one I Love, or should I wait a bit? Not so sure I could even talk to Declan, if by some miracle I were to find him. I keep praying he's not dead, nor something close to it.

I know this Abrams dude, because he developed *Fringe,* and I couldn't get enough. *Lost* hooked me from the very first second of the very first scene. I bought every season and Sawyer & Kate definitely need to go at it once in a while, just for the fun of it...yeah, too bad Doc.

Abrams is kinda like Chris Nolan (weird – that's the name of the lead character in my 1995 script, *The Gift*) (Are these things gentle co-incidences? I think not. I think intent and purpose. Maybe I think too much...Chris for our son and Nolan for LA, my best friend.) Anyhow, as the series twists and turns, I'm so involved with all the characters, I'm actually crying my eyes out when one dies or gets hurt or Can't Find Their Way Back Home....to the group, that is...thank you, Stevie Winwood. Fell in Love with you when I was eighteen and never fell out, but that's pie in the sky, so never you mind. Anyhow, sorta like me at this

106

particular point on my journey. I guess I'll find who I need to find, when I need to find them. I pray, anyway....
BHH/THINKING OUT LOUD IN MY DIARY AFTER JACK

DECEMBER 1970/IU/BLOOMINGTON/IN: Joe freaked me out, tonight – he was incredibly angry and I'm not sure why…well, yeah, I guess that's a lie. He says he's been my friend, my brother and now he wants to be my lover…and he wants it on *his* terms? What the heck does that mean??? I'm still virgin territory! I got news for him. He is not one of my three and I told him so. Hightailed it outta there, jumped in my MG and raced home – with him on my tail; it's okay, I can out-drive him. I learned to drive a manual in my sleep and that's the God's truth…no worries.

I screeched to a halt just this side of my apartment door and my hands were shaking when I unlocked it – no fear, just thinking what an unadulterated and arrogant bastard he is. The *nerve*! As I'm unlocking the door (damn thing sticks and we've asked the super to fix it, like a million times). Joe arrives and jumps outta his MG.

The door slowly sweeps across the (orange!) shag carpet and I move inside, trying my best to shut him out, but Joe is over six feet tall and has a powerful physique. He is powerful in this life – and, angry. Bad combo. I stand, quiet; stare him down, like a scolding mom.

His eyes shift to the floor, and I see that he's calmed, and all this stuff is racing through his mind and he knows, now, that he might have lost me altogether, if, that is, he ever truly had me – which, he did not. I am not the one for JFC, Jr. and he knows it. I double-dog dare ya knows it. At this point I had not, yet, met any of my Three. Declan would come first in five brief months, but I did not know that, then.

Sheepishly, he withdraws a small, wrapped gift box and hands it to me.
What's this, says I.
Christmas, says he.
I narrow my eyes and open the box – it's a leather MG key fob. (Be still, my heart…)
Oh, wow, you shouldn't have, says I.
I love you, says he.
No, you don't, says I. You just want what you want and I'm not giving. Get over it, Joe. You and I do not play well together. Go talk to someone. You need help and it's okay – Vietnam was hell, so no shame, there. I'm not qualified for this level of treatment, Love. Forget *us* and move on. Didn't you tell me your folks want you to marry that other girl, the local one? He shakes his head yes.
Then, go; go and marry her, says I.

Two weeks later I spot them cruising campus in his car. Somehow it almost broke my heart. Go figure. He was a hard one to let go. But I had to and so did he. Warriors to the end. But, JFC, Jr. and I were not done with one another quite yet. Next time it would be me chasing him and that hide and seek never did get resolved. Not to my liking, anyway.
BHH/POETRY FOLDER/1970/FIRE AND RAIN, MY SWEET LORD/FIRE AND RAIN

1981/TIBURON/CA/SAM'S ANCHOR CAFÉ: Can you believe I've never tasted guacamole?! My co-workers are appalled, but most of them live here and back east it's not a big thing.

108

Harry orders some – yeah, the same Harry who will later scare away Clint Eastwood just as he's getting down to the big flirt with me – everything's perfect…

The guac is really good and I can't figure what's wrong with the east coast…not having this food available is a crime! For sure!

I constantly scan the crowd to see if Declan is anywhere around – I just can't kick him out of my heart. I can't release him. Can't bury him, can't stop thinking about him and wondering if he's okay – alive and free? Every time I'm in CA – or IN – or, anywhere else for that matter.

God, let's just admit it: he had my heart from the very first moment and there is no denying it – from before we ever even met! What's *that* all about? I don't know. I know only this: I must find him and satisfy this need to see. Peggy March all over again. Flashback to 1963. See, we women folk were ingrained with these ideas of Prince Charming and following our man.

That's not how I'm thinking, though. Nope. I'm thinking all those times Declan and I were something to one another in many lives and in many places and in many different times – I'm thinking just how freaking connected we were and wondering if we still are.
 BHH/LOST/LOOKING FOR MY OTHER HALF

APRIL 7, 2016/BOCA GRANDE, FL/YESYESYES
I love affirmations and use them frequently. I find them to be uplifting and they help me nip it in the bud, when my ego rears its ugly head and tries to snatch the lead from my Spirit. If everything is genuinely perfect, then should we give up the fight for that which we desire, or want, or believe we are supposed to experience? No fuckin' way,

109

Man! Keep on fightin', Baby, and if you think for a second that everything's chiseled in stone, well, think again.

Declan and I are talking and I'm spilling my guts, mostly in emails. He told me how he stashes away the moments and people who have hurt him or in some way, in his mind, done him wrong: or, that he has harmed in whatever way. So, I have been shut away, caged in the darkness, kept in a place where no one (especially Declan) can see or talk with me. I am completely alone and he won't even allow me to mingle – to even think about mingling with any other memories. Ostracized and alone: sorrowful and lonely…

God, I Love you so, says he. Really Loved you once upon a time. And I know he means it. He meant it back then and he means it now. Last night, he says to me, Well I'm thinking I loved you so deeply once before, might as well see if it's still there - we do have a long history, don't we?

Hmmm…do we? Dear One, we will make a new history, together, for whatever time we decide to share. You have been in my heart and on my mind for over forty years. But you locked me away.
BHH/CALIFORNIA DREAMIN' IN BOCA GRANDE, FL

1885/WESTERN NORTH CAROLINA: Eileen and Matt are an item and I'm happy, too, because Matt has handed me an amazing travel journal about his last trip to Tibet and the Himalayan climb. He's bankable and if that keeps him around for a time, then I'm pleased – for Eileen and for me and Matt: nothing like old friends.

You know, there is more – much more to this than simply recurring energies of people – there are recurrences of places, too. Places generate, hold and encompass, sometimes, vast amounts of energy: threads of positive and negative energy just hiding, bouncing, floating, waiting, popping all over the place. Can you feel it? Feel that gentle, warm breeze? Who is that, I wonder? It's someone, I'd bet.

I'm going fly fishing tomorrow with Matt, so we'll be able to connect again, in this life, and share some thoughts about how this is all unravelling, this time. But nothing too, too weird; unless you want to count that odd looking thing flashing across the sky, but we all just pretend we don't see it. All is well.
BHH/ASHEVILLE/FOUND IN A HANDMADE LEATHER JOURNAL, EMBLAZONED WITH THE ANCIENT TRIQUETRA SYMBOL, and signed in clear/legible cursive script "MAHON O'MATHGHAMHAIN, 1885" THE BEAR

1994/SARASOTA/WITH CLARE AND JOE KENNEDY: Jack had surgery in Florida where he became ill, collapsed, and almost died. I flew down, gathered him from the hospital and drove us back to Tilghman Island; arranged for help and drove back to Florida to finish up our scheduled shows. Clare and Joe are like second parents to me and I love them more than I can express. I'm staying with them at their Longboat Key home.

The previous evening, Clare, Joe, and I had a lively discussion about our family histories – the Kennedys are the original ancestors of the O'Briens and O'Mahonys and I did not know that until Joe told me the stories. So, when Clare and I enter a bookstore and she spots a book of Irish names and suggests I get it, I do. I buy it and stuff it away, forgetting about it, as is oft my pattern.

Many years before, when Jack gave me a 'medicine name', a name which is considered a true and genuine name

111

reflecting a person's spirit, he decided upon "Bright Bear" because he saw me as a bright energy and we all know what a mother bear can be like; so, the name fit me to a T. I am that bear.

In 1990, Jack began making jewelry (this was after he became very well known for his hand carved decoys and holiday figures and we were invited to the White House where we met the Reagans) with me. I had started making necklaces a couple years, previous. When I asked him to join me, he did. We chose *Bright Bear Wearable Art – Bright Bear Treasures* – as our new company name.

About that same time, Jack suggested I take a screenwriter's course offered through one of the local Community College's continuing education programs. I felt restless and wanted to get back to my first love of writing. That wonderful class inspired me to take other writing classes, where I met amazing teachers – people who encouraged me to press on and keep writing. I ended up completing several movie scripts. The second screenplay I wrote was based upon a dream I'd dreamed in 1994 about Ire.

When I wrote out the dream, I remembered my name was Mahon (pr. Mann) and I was male. My wife was named Niamh (pr. Neev). Several weeks after I transcribed the story of the dream, I looked up the spelling of 'Niamh', because I wasn't sure if 'Neev' was correct – it wasn't and so I changed the spelling to the current and correct Gaelic: Niamh, which means BRIGHT and whose contemporary counterpart is Clare. Clare Kennedy and I believe in intent and purpose, and we saw it, clearly, in those wafts and wefts of the tapestry I was weaving – and, with her and Jack's help.

112

"Mahon" in ancient Gaelic and is the root word of my mother's family name: O'Mahony, which (you guessed it) means BEAR…everything's fuckin' perfect and those dots do connect…when we're patient and see things through to the conclusion.

Co-incidence?

What do you think?
SCRIBBLED IN THE BOOK OF IRISH NAMES THAT CLARE FOUND FOR ME. THERE ARE NO COINCIDENCES.

2012/EXCERPT: *NOTES FROM MOM:* "Yes, if you're an artist, or any kind of adventurous, creative, *interested* human, then you most definitely do not relish the thought of becoming bored. When our energy is high, we have only a small chance of boredom. Bored=ego thinking which, basically, means too much emphasis on ourselves and maybe not enough energy on others.

Energy surrounds all of us - we <u>are</u> energy. Every 'thing' in the world is energy. It's everywhere! Our personal energy emanates all around us: it shoots upward from the top of our heads, it vibrates out to our sides, it permeates down from our feet and rolls away from each of us, going ahead of us and trailing behind us. We might think no one can know what we're thinking or feeling, but there are those who can read us, because they read our energy.

We all *throw* energy. We may not even realize we do it, but it's a constant with humans. We project who we are with every heartbeat, every thought, each word and all our actions. We can't hide. What saves most of us is that most others are just too busy to be aware of what we're throwing

113

out there and so, we aren't found out. Think about it. How many people actually listen? How many *think*?

We are all very, very busy, from the moment we awaken until we lay our heads on our pillows – many of us keep going, even then. Some of us don't know where our turn off switch is – we can't stop thinking, worrying, debating, second-guessing, reliving, etc. Most of us are a freakin' mess - unable to engage, with some of us not really wanting to participate all that much.

Thought is energy. To those who take the time and exert the effort, thought/energy manifests itself as a substantial force, which can be felt and known by others – it's palpable. When people discover how powerful their energy is, and they use it, they're often described as being charismatic. They can use their charisma in positive and negative ways.

No one can hide – not really. (Seems like Declan can…) We might think we can, but there's someone out there, who will discover who we are: thoughts reach a certain critical mass and they're as visible as an arm or leg. Still, it depends upon whether or not anyone is aware enough to see it. Or to even look.

We've encountered people who are so joyous, so centered in Love that they seem to glow – they couldn't hide it if they tried. It shines out from them, sparkles around them and dances like a kinetic aura wherever they move. It's beauty and we know it when we see it.

We've also met people whose anger oozes about them and those closed off by a deep hurt. We've met, or know, people who seem like Ziggy, with his little rain cloud hovering just over his head. Let's face it – we've all been those people. But it's the dark and foreboding energy,

114

which pushes most of us away…thank God for the human angels, who can see through this negativity, hurt, ego drama and reach out a hand, lend an open heart or ear, to listen.

So, if you believe your thoughts are your own and are undetectable, unrecognizable, hidden and secret, well, think again.

Everything about you becomes your banner.

Take as much time choosing what your mind dwells upon, and within, and where your thoughts linger as you do when you chose what you wear, because your thought/energy fills the vacuum around you and becomes a part of you – it precedes your physical body and follows it. It's out there. You, the genuine you, cannot often hide. Before and behind, above and below, our thoughts weave a field of their own – a kind of ephemeral fabric, all around us: all of us. We embrace, or reject, long before we think we actually perform those actions. And we do it based upon the energy we sense or feel.

Our Truest Self exists as an energy wave: a detectable manifestation and extension of our organic self. So, try to Be Aware. Try to Think Carefully.

I need to think carefully: figure out where Declan would settle his energy, this time of his life…. married? Alive? Don't know. I will find him - come what may. BHH/2014/NFM/CAN'T READ THE MAP/EYES TOO FULL OF TEARS/HEART TOO FULL OF WONDER…I'LL TAKE WONDER, THIS TIME, PLEASE

1976/PARK HILLS, KY/MCGRAW-HILL REP FOR CINCINNATI/DAYTON: Jamaica and Mexico were game

changers, for me. If <u>those</u> places were wonderful, exciting and interesting, then I can only imagine Europe and Africa. I did not feel any past energy in either Jamaica or Mexico, so these were probably my first trips there. I have a strong feeling Euro/Afrique will be quite different – I'm pretty certain I've experienced past lives in both places. I hope I remember when I go and walk the earth. Hope I walk the earth, where once, I walked the earth...
BH/WRITTEN ON MCGRAW HILL STATIONARY AND FOLDED LIKE A LETTER/STASHED

1875? /HOW WOULD I KNOW? COTE D'IVOIRE:
Dey came 'gin, last night, in da middle a'night. Manage ta run/hide las' time – not so, dis time. Dey got six of us carryin' cages – cages holdin' many children and women. Da ones has full grown men, like me, hold fewer and so, we have a small share a'space. Won't allow da strongest ta do totin' – fer obvus reason'. I 'member when I travelled ta Eng-land as but a boy. Tot dey was sneaky buggers, den, as dey've proved ta be. Listen at yer voc when it talk to ya, at's all I ken say. Least I can sorta speak and understan' 'em – dey don't know dis dough. Sic wi' blud tox...swets/puke...reel sic...wi'da fevr.

Deir concept a'time is strange, ta me. I luk ta da Mudder and watch and lis'n and know what ta 'spect. Dey luk ta dials and needles and dey tink dey know nuff. Dey don. I frum dis dirt, now dey tie da cages down an' we go 'cross seas. Terble sic...mite di....dunno......
BHH/REMEMBERING IVORY COAST/FROM BEFORE/NOTE JOTTED IN DIARY/DATED/1987

APRIL 13, 2016/THE PLAN/TWO GEMINI BIRTHDAYS: It'll be 40 PLUS, yep, that's forty-PLUS years, on my birthday, this coming May 30th, that Declan first "bedded" me - popped my cherry, fucked my brains

116

out, had me, Loved me, shagged me, balled me, screwed me, banged me etc., etc...I was twenty and he was twenty-one (or would be soon). For me, it was like a dream – he was my very first lover and Love... and we did none of those crude and nasty sounding things – nonono: we made LOVE. Love is all you need.

It was a scary, exhilarating, confusing, Love-filled, heart-filled and spirit-filled time. I have never forgotten it. I never will. That day, my birthday, I spent with someone I knew Loved me, and I Loved him, from before we ever even met and would continue to do so, through eternity. We might not always find one another in each and every life; but we have enough to understand the importance of him to me and me to him. Amazing. That's all I can say. That's enough.

There will be no Dear Johns, face to face or otherwise. Not anymore. Even if we don't stay together, we will always stay together. I surrender. And I'm okay with that. No need to fight, ever again. My angels have angled their swords downward and lowered their shields. Me, too. No use fighting a thing – a feeling, which can't be battled. It's already won: the 'thing', the emotion, the feeling – it's trapped in my heart so deep, so hard I can't remove that hook.

But we'll see if either, or both, of us have the heart to do whatever needs to be done, for Love: Just for Love, Darlin' - if not, then we don't deserve it, anyhow, or maybe there's another Plan. Maybe I'm Amazed, Baby...for sure, I am amazed. Love on, Darlin'. Love on.

In 1994, when I had my angels channeled, Agathe told me to stop fighting. The time for fighting is over. Call the

117

Ancient Ones to you. The time is Now. The time is Now. The time is Now, says she.

Then, she explained that I'd been a warrior throughout most of my lives and it's time to stop. She said my heart was (literally) pierced by every weapon known to humankind – it had been struck by swords, knives, lances, bullets, arrows, pikes etc., etc....everything had, at one time or another, eventually killed me, it seemed. This life I am from the Key Harmonic Realm. Go figure...

I was also told that I've lived many lives into my nineties and longer: that my life, this time, was driven by Love and that I was having a bit of a hard time with letting go of the warrior memories. That a soul I Loved, deeply, had hitch-hiked with me this time and was making me confused and saddened. Agathe removed that one, thank goodness. I experienced immediate relief and weight shifting off me.

He/she was lodged in a hole in my heart.

Never leave holes in your heart because some energy will fly in - usually the one you don't really want or need.

I guess I can admit this; writers, truly, write for themselves and no one else. That's the God's truth. Yeah, Shakespeare was just as tickled as I am, when he finished a sonnet – don't you doubt it! I can just see him running down to ole Chris Marlowe's house and trying to show off, reading his poetry aloud with a smile that said, 'See, I always knew I was the better poet'. I would have loved to see Chris' expression!

But I can't. Long gone. I can, however, see my expression, or at least know it – some small part of it. I can see your expression, but it doesn't carry much weight, with me, unless you are here, in front of me…the big thing with me is energy and I don't often fail in recognizing <u>What It Is</u>, just like Mose Tolliver. That's another story.

I don't put much faith or trust in energy when I can't physically see you, or whomever. I guess that's why I'm not a Reiki Master. So, we all mingle our thoughts, our words and our actions; all our combined energies make up this world we all inhabit and call home.
Better be careful what we think, eh?
BHH/CHUMMIN' AWAY

The Love I Made, 1975
by Barbara Helvey Hughes

When I was young, my course yet laid
I did not care to see
That all the love I ever made
Rolled gently back to me.

In passion, pause, and steady flow
I prayed on bended knee
My prayers so loud, I could not hear
The love ebb back to me.

I searched for love - the price was dear
And this much I now see:
That all the love I ever made
Flowed always back to me.

In my lost soul the ache was deep
The longing sure and true
I was too young to know I keep
The love I gave to you.

It can't be caged, it can't be bought
Released, love must be free.
In innocence, my heart had thought
"It won't return to me."

How sad my youth's love was so blind
How sad I failed to see
That all the love I ever find
Out from the heart, the soul, the mind
Comes tenfold back to me.

Yes, Declan, I wrote this poem for you. Well, mostly for you, anyhow. For Dickie and you and Jack and all the rest. I guess we never truly stop loving the ones we've so loved. How can we?

This life has been so perfect. How can I possibly complain? I cannot. Will we come together again? Who can say? I had an amazing life with Jack and Chris, and everything is perfect – as it should be and as it was meant to be to help us arrive at this place. I've learned so much.

How many people ever experience, let alone even imagine, the depth/breadth of love I have known? I wonder how it is I have been so blessed. But I cannot question it – there are no answers to these kinds of questions. Still, I often wondered, what were you doing, Declan? Were you safe? Where were you? So, whatever happens, in the end, for us, will also prove perfect. Things always work out – they may not work out the way we hope or desire, but they always work out and sometimes all we need is distance from the event, to figure out just how perfect each and every moment unfolds. Truly.

Of course, had I known, then, that you had a family, I would have simply crossed you off my heartlist – probably placed you, ever so gently, into my own locked box, where you could do no emotional harm to me. As it was, I left you out, picked you up, turned you around, inspected you, probed you under my mind's electron microscope...examined you – the why/how/when/where/what of it all. Always, I Loved you. Always. Was that enough? Yes. I've come to understand that Love is always enough. It is for me, anyway. I can't answer, for you.

Comin' up for air.....
BHH/2016/THINKING FULL-CIRCLES ARE BEST FOR CROP WATCHERS

1977/COTE D'IVOIRE/LAYIN' ON THE DOCK: I awakened last night to find The General (Emeka Ojukwu) sitting in a chair, next to my bed, reading. When I awoke, he informed me I'd been lost for several days, but they had kept constant watch to make sure I was still among the living and the doc had been there many times, to check my vitals. I was so incredibly weak; I couldn't speak to the dear man - just smiled and returned to Never-Never Land. He whispered, "Now you're African, Barbara." I opened my eyes and saw his smile, beaming across that beautiful face of his. I smirked and whispered, "I don't want to be African....but, thanks...." He chuckled.

This morning, Stella helped me up and I stood, awkwardly, on uneasy legs, before taking a step. She has ****** bring me a cup of tea and a piece of dry toast – couldn't eat the toast, but one bite. Tea was really good. After an hour or so, I announced I must bathe. (I'm certain a kind of relief washed over her face – no pun intended...) The maid needs to strip my bed and clean up, so I slowly head for the walk-in shower – and I do mean walk in: takes up half of the enormous bathroom.

I stand and allow the tepid water to rush over my tired and emaciated body. I barely recognize myself. I've lost so much weight it doesn't register at first. As I run soapy hands along my skin, I realize just how debilitating these tropical diseases really are – my flesh is limp and there's very little colour to my skin – very little *life*.

I'm twenty-seven years old – in my prime – and I feel like a ninety-year-old must feel (in my imagination, at least) (Yeah…I remember). I ache in places I didn't even know I had. My <u>bones</u> ache…my skin, the muscles, tissues, everything physical feels awful. My *hair* hurts! I simply want to surrender and go back to bed. Even the "HELP" I attempt to scream, inside my head, comes off sounding wimpy. I can't find the strength to say the word. I should be grateful, beyond belief, that I'm standing in the shower, with no help – believe me, I am.

Stella has to go into the closest town and I've dressed myself, but I'm freezing. It's probably eighty degrees outside and I feel like I'm in the Artic, so I pull out every sweatshirt and long-sleeved shirt I brought on this trip and yank out another pair of blue jeans, pull them on and wrestle into all the shirts. No kidding, I put all of it on and I'm still cold.

I stumble out to the dock – I'm the only one here, except for the servants, and there are plenty of them milling around. Jeez, The General had the pool filled for me! I shiver, just thinking of it and walk on, arrive at the dock, and gaze out to the lagoon. The President of the Ivory Coast lives across the lagoon from The General and Stella. I allow that thought to settle into my brain, shake my head and wonder how the hell did a small-town Indiana farm girl ever land here. Amazing. Ain't life grand?

Suddenly weariness overwhelms me and I collapse onto the dock, curl in a fetal position and the fleeting thought of what I must look like to the house servants (crazy white woman) flutters through my brain. I initiate the short trek toward slumber...sink fast....relax and allow my lethargy and illness to hook me and carry me away. Softly, quietly I walk the road away from reality, into a beautiful dream, where an exquisite voice calls a chant to me, beckons me to him. My feet each weigh about five hundred pounds, so the going is woefully slow, but at least I move...I think I move....my eyelids quiver and, finally, open to slits: through which I think I see a canoe. Yes!

I hear the dip of the oar into the water, the pull and the rise of each stroke as the canoer faintly sings the lovely chant.

I realize how rude I'm being, laying there without acknowledging just how marvelous this man's voice is and how grateful I am to hear it, to see him glide by ever so softly. Is this a dream? I pull myself up - a smile spreads across his magnificent face and I smile right back, clasp hands, bow my head and whisper Namaste; my version of 'I see the God in you'. My waist long blonde hair is soaking wet and I'm still shivering from the ice crystals raging in my blood, pumping through my half-frozen veins. I collapse back onto the dock and watch him through barely more than slivers of vision.

Next thing I recall, I'm in bed still fully clothed and still freezing. Will this never end? Am I to die, in Afrique? Won't be the first time. Won't be the last. Sailing away.......OMG – will I just die here in Afrique, without ever seeing Declan, again?

123

BHH/BARELY LEGIBLE IN DIARY, LABELLED
AFRIQUE/VAIL, COLORADO/MCGRAW HILL
BUSINESS MEETING/AUGUST/1977/ON THE
ROAD AGAIN

2016/APRIL 17/FLORIDA, BUT CALIFORNIA
DREAMIN': Namaste, Dear One.

I know I shouldn't be writing you this email, but I have to
let you know how insistent you are, in my heart and
thoughts. You woke me up at 5:30 - I felt your hands roam
all over me - I turned to kiss you, but you aren't with me
yet. Then I remembered that it will be only a moment until
we finally meet again after all these years.

When I see you, Love, I do want to be able to see <u>only</u> you.

Some mornings/days are more difficult than others. This
morning was a challenge, because I did *feel* you...some
mornings I can quiet myself and center you in Love and
place you in my heart and spirit, knowing you will be there
with me, calm and peaceful all day.... other days I feel an
urgency - almost a frantic need for you- over and over all
day long and well into the night. I can't calm myself, like
your energy is here and constantly reaching for me and I
want it, so I find it almost impossible to release you and get
on with my day.... that's when I try to write the most. If I
didn't have that release, if I couldn't let go of you and do
what I need to do right now.

The gallery has been slow, but this is the kind of business
where things can change on a dime. Someone can walk in
and turn everything around. This is the time of year when
that always happens. It's just the waiting, again...but that
waiting allows me many months off every year.

Yesterday, when you told me you were fencing all day (that means a couple things to me... did you know I fenced in college?) (Like, with a foil...) I almost envied you the physicality of it. I hope you were so tired that you really slept deep and well, last night. Just to be tired on that level might give me some comfort at this point. I love to be tired, in my bones. There's such release in it and such vitality - it makes me realize how alive I still am.

You will make me realize how alive I am, and I will do that, for you...just thinking about it makes me smile. I hope you're smiling, right now, with me. One of these days I should try to describe how every part of my body feels when I think of you. I've felt this way forever with you, Declan. It's sort of like an electrical current pumping through each capillary, every vein and artery - like it's running in my blood and feeding each organ, every teeny, tiny part of my physical body, but then, it grows and becomes so much more - an energy that pulses into my brain and into my heart - the vital physical parts of me and finally it settles in my chest, where I believe my spirit resides...there have been many times when I do actually feel you, physically, touch me. I love your hands - I remember them. I love every part of you. I'm done in.

Earth to Barbara.

Today, my morning wishes for you are that you awaken in comfort and peace, joyful to begin your day. That you are surrounded by positive energy all day - you embrace it and carry it with you into all you think, say and do. Another hope is that you reach for me - I'm right there, next to you. Take me in your arms and hold me. Hold me so close we melt together, Declan, so close we become as one. That's what I feel every morning to some degree, and I hope you

125

feel it, too, and that it makes you feel phenomenal...full and joyful...how I Love you.

Be well in all aspects of you and your day, today.
My love is with you, in spirit, but you and I are very physical beings, too (no sense in wasting a gift, huh?!). Declan, reach for me today. The best part of me is already there, with you. I Love you, Dear One. Have a glorious day.
Barbara
BHH/FOUND IN DECLAN NIALL'S EMAIL FILE

1994/ST. PETERSBURG, FL: I'm in Florida, alone, and doing craft shows with our jewelry every weekend. I make my necklaces etc during the week – I've overtaken Bubba's dining room and God bless him, he's so patient with me.

I rent a movie, called *Blown Away*, with Jeff Bridges (Jimmy Dove – the dove, my sacred symbol) and this song comes on – *Return to Me* by October Project – you know, there are times when I just wish I could turn this stuff off. Everything, literally everything means something, to me. I'm on symbolic overload.

So, I'm in the middle of deciphering a dream and morphing it into a script called yeah, you got it – *The Golden Thread*. It's about a life I lived in 10th century Ireland, as a king of my clan. Jack was Niamh, my wife. Out of the flippin' blue, Jack calls that night and says, Barb, you know I waited a thousand years for you, this time - of course I startle, but continue the dream telling, when he cuts me off and says, I know, Babe, then he finishes telling me about the dream he, obviously, shared with me, because he told me every freakin' detail.

Okay, Alice, I'm jumpin' – I'm all in!

126

Hand over the DRINK ME bottle!

I'm listening to *Return to Me*, now, in 2016 and I have to wonder...
BHH/SCRIBBLED ON THE BACK OF <u>THIS</u> EDIT, 2016, MAY 4TH – CAN'T FIND MY WAY HOME, BUT THOUGHT I DID...

2016/MAY16/PLACIDA, FL: Wow, less than two weeks until we reunite, after forty some years of living our lives, without one another, raising our families, being spouses, parents, friends – sort of scary but mostly happy anticipation about this.

Listening to Ed Sheeran. I'd never heard of this singer, until Declan emailed me one of his songs. What have I been doing for all these years? Care-giving, mostly. It's okay. I'm catching up. I love this "X" CD. Wonderful melodies and great lyrics, and the guitar, so sweet and painful; almost like ole Ed wrote them just for us. And, no, I won't find another place 'to let my heart collide' with anyone else, Dear One.

The song *One* gave me goose bumps, because I remember 'stumbling home drunk' and being so completely unbalanced and lost after I returned from DC. But I now know a bit of what was going on in your life, Declan and I better understand it. When Ed says "We'll be strangers if we see this through" he is right on. Still hurts, but since I do believe that everything is perfect, it goes almost without saying (but, I'll say it) that the life we each lead was the life we needed to lead for our individual, and co-joined, spiritual development. Had we been together, back then, with all the craziness, we might not even have a chance to be together, now.

My gut instinct, although I'm already in love with you and have been since 1971, is to go slow, be thoughtful and deliberate. You have been woven into the very sinews of my heart - you are my heartstrings: one of the most important stones in the foundation of my understanding of Love. I know that seems weird, since we senselessly broke one another's hearts. But this life is merely one in a long, long strand we've been weaving for, well, for**ever.**

Yours and mine – those are the Golden Threads – as are Jack's and mine, mine and Chris', yours and all the ones you love and all those we have both loved and still love… and, yes, I AM all in, in every way. I believe we have a tapestry and I know it is unbelievably gorgeous! Faith. Yes.

Even though this sense of urgency has returned with somewhat a sense of, well, urgency – it is not a negative thing this time. We get what we need when we need it. It would be wonderful to live the final phase of our lives, encompassed by our love for one another. I'm living expectantly, but with no expectations - as much as is humanly possible.

I can't wait to see you. To hold you. Intent and purpose. Will we find our way, My Love? I have no answers: all I can do is believe that whatever happens fulfills something for each of us.
BHH/SLOUCHING TOWARD COLORADO WITH A BANJO IN MY HAND/SCRIBBLED ON SHEET MUSIC/OH SUSANNA!

NEW SUNSIGN/DECLAN'S SUNSIGN/MY SUNSIGN/GEMINI – MAY 21, 2016: We slipped into Gemini last night and I felt the earth move. Everything moved. Now I am home. Full on full moon tonight. Can it get any better?

I loved your smell. It's one of the things I most remember about you – that beautiful, earthy smell you carry, like you just came in from plowing the back forty and you're looking at me, hungry, like you never saw anything like me. Once upon a time, Jack loved me insanely and anyone who genuinely knew and understood him knew that – our synergy was wildly perfect, wonderfully weird and finely honed, even when it might have seemed to others, to be so alarmingly imperfect. I loved him just as fierce, because I love fierce. Period.

But for now and in this present, I want to melt into you…lose track of time, of place, of emotion and thought - just be with you, a part of you. God, is this too much for you, now? I know once upon a time, when we were much, much younger it would not have been; but now? I don't know; you must tell me, please. Talk to me, share with me. It isn't that I expect you to be twenty-one, again, and on the ready every time our eyes meet. I understand age's nasty jokes believe me. But my hands can still roam and feel; my eyes can still drink you in; my mouth can still lick and kiss and moan; my ears still listen to your heart thump inside your chest and your life-breath inhale/exhale. I breathe you in with every one of my own gasps as your mouth finds my pulse. Mercy, how I have missed you, Love.

And not only your physicality, Declan; no, it's not simply *that* - it is every atom of your energy – every molecule of you that I have yearned for, missed with every molecule of my own being. I believe we were truly one being, split in two and forever attempting to find our other half. Well, Baby, our hunt is over. We did the impossible and we found one another very early in our lives. Doesn't matter, in the present, who walked away first, second or third - what is genuine, in this moment, is that the universe in its infinite

129

wisdom, allowed the two of us to locate each other, reach out, be available and try this Love back on for size, now, entering our final years. What will we find?

And, Declan, I was your home as you were mine. If it works, again, that's the wonder. If not, there's wisdom to be gained in all experiences. It's just so simple, so perfect, so pure that sometimes it takes each of us most of our lives to acknowledge it, accept it, embrace it and become One with it.
BHH/ONE LOVE

22MAY2016/ONE WEEK TO GO: Okay, Heart, we have one week and when we spoke on the phone, last night, I practically swooned and I have never swooned in my entire life. I've been told I have a lot of the anima/animus going this life, this time around; passion so fierce it scares some males away. Glad you never balked, because that tells me volumes about you and who you are, not only this time, now, but in our past…. you get it…you get me and that makes me want to, even more, have an "I'm dropping my shields" kinda attitude. Mostly, I've had to raise the ray guns and fire at will; been fortunate to find three souls, this time, who don't mind (so much, anyhow) the power I wield, because they're likely to be just as powerful, if not more. It's not a contest, it's just a long, long strand unravelling out and creating the universe, as we know it.

Like you said, second guessing doesn't do either of us any good and we are who we are. Can we retrieve those strands and make something out of them? We will both know as soon as we're in each other's presence – we both read energy really well and especially each other's, so there is no hiding. We will be face to face, heart to heart, Soul to Soul…everything to everything and the only ones who can fuck this up is us.

130

You are the biggest obstacle to this, YOU, because you hid me away and seldom, if ever, thought of me. I, on the other hand, wove you in and out of my thoughts, my memories, my desires and my intentions for many years. I never let you go, believing we had time, and we would rejoin. My experience tells me that most folks just don't morph into someone else all that easily or without some motivation – our 'core' remains pretty stable and pretty much the same; but widens, deepens, becomes more intense….we *become*…become the Souls we intended to become when we arrived in this time and place. And, I recognize your core – it mirrors my own: halves of a whole. The question, then, becomes are we willing to take the leap and re-join - become one or do we play it easy and safe and not allow any messiness? Stay on our own? Alone? It's genuinely the only way we've ever been, anyhow.

I sure can't project the outcome of any of this, just as I can't predict how I might feel when I'm in front of you, staring into your eyes and energy and Love. But I don't need to and I don't want to. That compulsion does not exist, for me. I will wait it out, with the faith that what happens is in everyone's best interest and will assist us on our journey, whether we walk together or apart. I have no doubt we will find one another, again; but next time might be a long, long time coming. Especially if we aren't grateful for all we've been gifted, this time…the road goes ever on and on, huh?

Thirty miles, Heartbeat - that's all that separated us all those years we were growing up back in Indiana…thirty fucking miles. I can't even think of it anymore. Wears me out. Yeah, here we go.
BHH/THERE ARE WORDS/ELOQUENT, SHARP, DESCRIPTIVE WORDS – 1966 POEM/COULDA BEEN 4 U

1979/MARRAKECH/TOO LITTLE, TOO LATE: Since I didn't make it to Morocco with you, back in 1971, I figured I may as well go, now, and see if I can pick up your trail. Eight years? Of course, I don't. Pick up your trail, that is. I keep going places I think you'll be, or maybe I'm reading it all wrong – maybe you did go here, maybe you did walk these narrow, winding streets, hide out in some elusive rug bazaar and stay stoned on hash or mind-fucking opiates. Me, I swiggin' down mint tea like there's no tomorrow and I'm getting buzzed off that - fuck the opiates. I can't find you and, in all probability, I'm not supposed to find you – yet. Have to wonder where the hell this is going.

I can't even wrap my brain around any of this. If there *is* intent/purpose in this charade, I'd just love to have a clue.

God, where the hell are you, Declan? I took on an entire other territory, when I worked for WHF (SciAm) that included Indiana, just so I could go back to Bloomington several times a year and try to pick up your trail; that was in 1980 and you were long committed by then, but I knew it not.
BHH/DAISY BOUND GEMINI DIARY ENTRY

25MAY2016/FAITH: We cannot trust if we have no foundation of faith. Faith paves the way for wonderful, Loving emotions and experiences to enter our lives. Without genuine faith, trust cannot exist and the precursor to faith and trust, is Love. None of the positive forces (energies) can exist without Love. Love changes our entire beings and enhances all aspects of Who We Are. We change, because of Love, influenced by Love, energized by Love. Love is a certain wavelength and that energy impacts all it approaches and touches. Buddha, Jesus and The

Beatles – they by Mick Kagger and Mick Taylor all said it. I
say it. All you need is Love. For sure.
21OR3TO6/POWER NUMBERS ALL…PRINTED IN
MAGIC MARKER ON THE BACK OF FLEETWOOD
MAC RUMOURS CD – NEXT TO "YOU MAKE
LOVING FUN"

EVE/25MAY2016/SIGNS: Seldom write an entry before
bed but have been thinking about you and hoping you feel
well – healthy. Someone asked me to post a painting of J's
on FB, so I did. Answered some messages and got off as
fast as I could. Sometimes, when nothing's shaking at the
gallery I feel as if I'm glued to the banality of those pages.
My choice, I know. I might return, yet, tonight: can't dance.
But, to think about Jack - well, my heart actually aches. I
need relief: there you are. Here I am.
SWING AWAY MERRILL
SWING AWAY AT THOSE SIGNS, BABY/BREAK 'EM
DOWN
KEEPTHEALIENSATBAY
PRINTED ON THE FIRST WRITE OF THIS STORY

26MAY2016/IN A TIME WARP AND CAN'T GET
OUT/WAITING TO FLY TO DENVER TO SEE YOU/
LATER: Namaste, Dear One.
I'm sitting here listening to one of my very favourite singers
(recently added to my list, because of you - I'd never heard
of him, before you shared *Thinking Out Loud* with me) Ed
Sheeran and thinking about how he plays the guitar on *I'm a
Mess.* It's very sensual to me, when he gets to the part
where he begins the chorus *See the flames inside my eyes*...there's
a beat and a rawness that makes me crazy. Seriously, it
actually has a physical effect on me: it excites me and makes
me want you. So, of course I listen to it all the time! It just
occurred to me that it reminds me of really emotional
Flamenco music - classical guitar.... *Bloodstream* is the other

one that gets me going, but that's probably just a flashback to my early hippie days...better forgotten, for me. Again, it's the sensual beat of the drums in that one – and, also, it's the way he plays the accompanying guitar - like his fingers dance along the strings with no more effort than it takes for a butterfly to beat its wings...just so incredibly beautiful it almost makes me weep.   Sort of a 'rock me baby' beat. I imagine being in your arms when I hear this one. Just gently swaying.

Yeah, there is a deep sadness and loneliness in that song...a sort of confession...very intimate, yet carries a sense of isolation, too. Blue. My favourite colour...

Wow...I didn't expect that, this morning, but I am feeling very alert and excited, so I get it.
I'm feeling very plugged in - to everything.
I will probably write more, later.
Always, you're in my thoughts, in my Love, in my heart - you're everywhere.

I want to be where you are. I have to be somewhere, because Jack is not here and, yet, I am and I want to fulfill, live out my intentions. That is my imperative, my goal, my desire.
Love,
B
THE GOLDEN THREAD – ALL IN/ FOR REAL THIS TIME/ALMOST ILLEGIBLE IN DIARY BARBARA TOOK WITH HER TO DENVER TO MEET DECLAN

2016/PLAYLIST FOR DENVER TRIP: Now, evening and we have only Friday/Saturday and our travel day of Sunday to slog through. (*Moonlight Mile* by Jagger and Taylor)

Okay…listening to the Stones, *Moonlight Mile* and it just knocks me out......the sweet guitar on this song intro.

Yeah...*nights passin' slow* here - how 'bout there?

This is the kind of song I also want to write: not just love songs....we've both had such **lives**, huh? There's gotta be some great material in there!

I am just living to be lying by your side…(how true)
I mean, who says that shit? *I'm just about a moonlight mile on down the road*?! Meaning? Everyone discovers their own.

What amazing poetry.

The first time I heard it; it blew me away - every aspect of it. Still does. That album came out right before we got together...April, 1971

I'm riding down your moonlight mile...

Then the guitar comes in - you know, insistent and hard, right on the coattails of the drums then all the other instruments.... then Mick's rough, raw voice...c'mon, this is a freakin' brilliant song!

Oh I am sleeping under strange, strange skies - I remember that: bet you do, too.

No I don't have to fill every moment with the sound of my own voice or thoughts. I just feel particularly lonely and maybe a bit vulnerable, in this moment. For those of us who know we have been both genders in our many lives, we understand.

Anyhow, I *am* a writer, so, I write...and write....and write...

135

I'm thinking about you and feeling that feeling start to creep up my spine - you know that tingly feeling in my tummy; that sort of lustful, melting feeling that pools there, that Witchy pull of the moon and it just was a full moon, too.
Love,
B
Wow, what a muse you've become for me.
MOONLIGHT MILIN' IT BACK TO 1971/WRITTEN DELIBERATELY ON BIG STICKER FOR THE STICKY FINGERS GUYS/U KNOW WHO I MEAN?

LATER 3AM/4AM/ETC:
Startled awake and I'd swear you were just holding me – holding fast to me.

I think it happened when I lost my tether. I walked away, you walked (flew) away and for some intuitive reasons it just wasn't our time to walk side by side, eh?

So, when I hear a song like *Moonlight Mile*, it all rushes back to me…. my emotional tsunami.

Fuckin'a: we were only twenty and twenty-one, for God's sake. And even though you were no longer in my life, you still were my life. We might walk away but we can never, ever *truly* walk away. Not from the promises we made pre-Earth.

Free-fall time and it just won't stop. It echoes in that sweet, painful guitar at the very beginning of *Moonlight Mile*, with ole Mick humming out those chords. Arrows fired right at my ole heart.

What else is new?

Strange days and dark, dark nights. The mind-altering situations: just to forget you. It's such a simple thing to forget someone, right? Yeah…right. Halves of wholes are seldom successful at that particular assignment.

I always wonder Why the fuck meet up at all, if we have to WALK THE FUCK AWAY?! Yep; *Then You Can Tell Me Goodbye*. Gotta Love The Casinos….

And not look back….no, no, don't dare look back. Eyes bleed out and heart explodes: what the hell, it's just a body, anyway….like George MacDonald says – You don't HAVE a soul. You ARE a soul. You HAVE a body. He figured it out. Then, he told us.

We just don't listen…can't hear…too busy humming or belting out *Moonlight Mile*.

It's even worse when I hear Quicksilver do Bo Diddley's *Who Do You Love* or *Just for Love* or *Fresh Air* or McCartney singing *Maybe I'm Amazed* or well…you get it. I couldn't listen to any of them for years. *Presence of the Lord/Can't Find My Way Back Home/It's Too Late/Reason to Believe/Me and Bobby McGee/Love Her Madly/*the list goes on and on for the tunes that shot me back there, you know - back to that pain.

I couldn't look at it: finally, I just set it on fire and walked away.

Think maybe I drank myself into oblivion, then had to decide to either face it down or just die. I drew my sword and cut the fucker's head off. Then, I started back. Wow, long journey, Baby.

Here I am. There you are.

Here's the newsflash: I'm walking forward, and I might just walk backwards, so I CAN LOOK AT IT – see every bit of it! I refuse to walk away from anything or anyone for the remainder of this life.

I'm walking that moonlight mile and every other fucking mile that runs out ahead of me. Moon, sun, rain, sleet, fog – yeah, I'll walk right through it and I don't care what the hell is on the other side – I wanna see it!

Blow me away. Do your worst.

My shoulders fire up, and the tension can be unbearable at times. At least, now, I've released the fear. Cut that cord (chord?)

Compulsions – can't stop – have to be there, do it, face it, be one with it – it all belongs to all of us, we just don't see it that way – yet. Maybe some of us never will....

Ask me how many times I can listen to *Moonlight Mile* – how many times can I sing it with gut wrenching clarity? Go ahead – ask me. You don't want to know.

My friend was here and the question he had was this: what is it that attracts me to these certain-kind-of- characters? You know - the bad boys or the creatively driven, live-on-the-edge guys, this life? I think it's familiar to me – what I've been in many other lives/who I've been/the path I chose. Yeah, so fuck 'em if they can't take a joke.

I mean, we don't have warriors anymore – not really. Not "I'm lookin' you in the face and I'm raising my sword to sever your jugular" kinda warriors. Not <u>righteous</u> warriors. End of story. Walk away.

We just have *feed the greed warriors*, in this time/place.

We've all *done* the warrior gig and probably many times in many lives….what? You don't remember that one, huh? Think harder.

It's probably the reason why, with me, the physical is so important. I remember how brief it all is: all those lives - all in the blink of an eye. The tactile nature of a hug, of touch, of holding someone close – even a perfect stranger – makes everything easier, somehow. It's where we close the connection and well, *connect*.

I had to get the compulsions under control, because any compulsion, out-of-control is just a bad habit. Lack of discipline. Lack of tactics.

I lived a huge part of my life with Jack and he leaned on me – I leaned on him and we taught one another a lot of of lessons. Not sure we were particularly interested in learning many of them, but knew we had to: so, I put my head down and shoulders up and walked that road.

I swear to God, sometimes I can't believe I survived it. Wasn't sure I would on many occasions. Those were some lonesome valleys, some scary stuff: especially knowing what I knew about the Love I had - Jack. Sometimes, that path was far, far worse than battling perceived 'enemies'. You know – the physical ones, hundreds of years ago. When Woody and Mississippi John says you got to walk that lonesome valley all by yourself – they mean it. It's True.

Jack knew he was leaving and the farther away I get from his actual leaving the more I understand that he knew. Every day it was something - a confession, a soliloquy, a thank you, a declaration of Love…every day for the weeks preceding his death, he made the short trek from his studio to mine or from his bed to the front porch, where I often write.

Jack chose his words thoughtfully, carefully – like a surgeon, he filleted the English language to his benefit. He was concise. To the point. He made an impact.

He generally provided me with the exact word I needed to complete a thought, a poem, a script idea.

He couldn't spell worth shit and his writing was atrocious, but he was fuckin' brilliant. Really fuckin' brilliant and in his unique way. Some folks didn't see it; but I was *with* him, for years when we created stuff together, 24/7 - so, I <u>did</u> see it, yeah - I saw that brilliance.

I saw <u>Jack</u>. Or, so I thought. I believed I knew every atom, every cell, every spark, thought, inspiration, jealousy, desire, need, freak out, vision. I knew Jack on every possible Spiritual, physical, intellectual, emotional and mental level. I believed it.

I did not.

Awake and alert and engaged and connected, he was simply amazing. Except when he was not.

We all have our limits.

Yes, there were times I knew Jack better than he knew himself, whether he was awake and in this time zone or settled in the awake/sleep zone tripping out there on one of Jupiter's moons. And I don't mean drug-induced. Jack didn't genuinely need drugs. He couldn't *be* in a place without my shadow right there, dancing with him…I mean,

140

how many humans get the opportunity to be <u>so</u> connected
to other energies in one life?

Jack….Good journey, Love. I release you, completely. And
I, surely, Loved you.

Melodies
by
Barbara Helvey Hughes

Out there:
Out beyond the distant, farthest grey blue ridge
Silent mists rise
Track forward, evaporate, reveal increasingly intense
Blue, blue, blue.

Along now exposed graceful curves
Shadowed crevices and lightened heights
Hum lyrical.
Pool and cascade away from almost human, reclining forms:
Gently, gently, gently.

Beneath roan risen rocks
Weathered by wind, singed by sun, ravaged by rain, fluted
by fire
A breeze quickens.
I intone this Indian trail, alone.
Breathe. Breathe. Breathe.

Your Ancient Ones tug my Spirit core; unravel my passions.
Puncture my aura.
I embrace their sigh.
My Ancient Ones murmur against the pulse throbbing at
my wrist, my throat:
Beckon, skin to Earth, along wiser trails.

141

Now, cathedraled sacred stones chant, harmonize with
wind.
Now, ancestor's tears fill bubbling, rushing streams.
I hear your breath whisper against the nape of my neck.
I feel you float toward me - spin your light about me.
Your forest scent fills my lungs.

I see you - the melody of you - skip and twirl, leap and
crouch:
Wait.
Your taste fills my bones: so familiar.
So absent.
So forever.

I am here. You are not.
Understand, Dearest:
The symphony of Love so ingrained within my energy
Has surrendered you to the stars. You await rebirth.
Yet, I travel on…grateful to have sung with you, but
Knowing I must continue my song.

Now, to be readying to see you, Declan, in the flesh and
after all these long, long years seems almost Kafkaesque.
I've been sitting at this computer for three hours, thinking
and writing; reliving and looking back - something I know
you do not want or like to do, Love. If we can't face the
pain, how in the world can we understand or be grateful for
the joy? But, wow, I've thrown so much at you and, for the
most part, you stood ground when I let it fly. The twice
you faltered, cut and run; well, they were short-lived and I
felt like drowning myself a couple times.

No worries. The pain overwhelms sometimes, huh? Just
the fact that you have the desire to meet – you demand we
meet – you would have been here two months ago, if I
hadn't insisted upon waiting. You're in my heart, in my

soul, my mind. As I said, before: we are strands of the very same Golden Thread and we've been weaving this cloth for eons. Strong. I'm hoping this is one strong Love. Is it possible to have more than one, in one life? I believe it.

What are the big lessons as I see them, this life? Forgiveness, for sure. Letting go, a close second, for me. Patience. Faith. It all returns to Love. Always. All ways. What are yours? Are they the same as mine or have you had others that I didn't get? It all goes back to Love. It always does…always.
THE GOLDEN THREAD – THE STORY, NOT THE SCRIPT/IT'S ALL ILLEGIBLE TO ME

5/29/16/OXFORD HOTEL/DENVER: Declan, you just entered my room and I startle, because I don't recognize your energy or anything about you and even though I saw your photo, I just can't fit you into my brain. You are unrecognizable to me. I'm completely, and quietly, freaked. That's what expectations get us. My energy is all over the place and so is yours and it probably wasn't such a great idea that neither of us slept last night; but, hell, we couldn't help it, we were just so wired and excited. I'm staring at a stranger. Why are you hiding from me? Protecting your self? What the fuck's going on?
I PROMISE, I am TRUE. Let me in. Let me see you.

The Promise, 1975
By
Barbara Helvey Hughes

You shine on gilded wing
Forever,
Never stirring more than a breath away.
The part of me that holds you high above
The others, wanders restless –
Alone.

143

Smile, Lover.
I, too, am a soaring bird
Eagre to escape the menace.
Free.
Once in my life,
Free.

*FREEDOM'S JUST ANOTHER WORD FOR NUTHIN'
LEFT TA LOSE*/SCRIBBLED ON A BIG BROTHER
AND THE HOLDING COMPANY ALBUM, DATED
1969/WHERE THE HELL'S BOBBY WHEN I NEED
HIM????

9/29/2015/NC CABIN/ALONE AFTER JACK LEFT:
For the past couple days, I've had the distinct feeling I've
experienced all this before and, many times. I'm *very* serious
– this sense of déjà vu overwhelms me. Stops me in my
tracks. Thank goodness my memory's getting worse,
because I don't think I want to have this gripping at my guts
for the remainder of my life. Maybe I just want to forget.

Tuck and roll, Baby. Tuck and roll. Thanks, Julie.

What I'm beginning to realize is just how many moments I
DO feel I've been through something, before, but I ignore
it, shake it off, pretend it's not there, persistently knock,
knock, knockin' at my door – not heaven's…no, no,
no…*mine*! Why? Can't face it, why? Don't want to think
about it? Don't truly believe it? Too afraid to believe it? Too
lazy?
Too afraid?
Too afraid?
Too afraid?

144

Jack sensed it too. It was simply way too 'convenient' for us to be so deeply synchronized in this life, so synergistic even at the beginning when we'd first met. But I've found in this life that there are many people I have that with and it can't be a co-incidence with all of them; not with those memory vapors trailing behind each and every one of them. There are no accidents, no mistakes. We do not mis-step into mistakes: we are not in a movie - this is the real deal, here, folks.

Declan? For sure - I knew it with him – he was the first? The first in many, many of my experiences – our shared experiences...you know the ones...the ones we're afraid to talk about...scared to share with 'friends', lest they think, "Wow, this chick's certifiable." But these intuitions have taunted me since I was a kid. I simply didn't know enough, didn't have enough experiences to even have a clue. But it was there, with Dec, from the very first time I felt his energy as he watched me, but I couldn't see him...just felt him...then, when Mandy Rainwater introduced us and our energies arced and jumped between us....it was always there...I'm not so sure he remembers, now, after so many years: after so many years of absence. But I do. I feel it, still. I see it in my mind's eye, still. I know it...still. I taste it, just like I still taste him.

We've all been here before and even if Crosby, Stills, Nash and Young hadn't sung a song about it, we (some of us) would still come to it and still believe it. We just don't want to think about it, after all, why mull over what ifs - things not provable?

I'm looking out over the hidden ridgeline. The fog lays in thick with very little visibility. Sort of like how foggy my brain and emotions feel, right now. I enjoy the fog. I do not enjoy this figurative fog. Never have liked/wanted to lose control over my thinking.

We're not blinded by anything, as long as we don't need only our eyes in order to see. Everything is much more than it seems: deeper, wider, more complex, more beautiful.

A twig just snapped. Who's out there, by the edge of the woods? We're born, we live, we die, we're born again. I can't breathe. Maybe the fog is trying to suffocate me. Breathe, Barbara, breathe.

Help me understand.

Jack and I taught one another so much and so well, even if we did kick and scream against those lessons, much of the time...Warriors, STILL. Always.
SCRIBBLED ON THE INSIDE OF *SHAMBALA, THE SACRED PATH OF THE WARRIOR* by Chögyam Trungpa

OCTOBER 23, 2015/ROSY MORNING/CABIN'S SUNRISE: This morning the rose-coloured light was so thickly saturated, it seemed as if I could wade into it, like water. I walked out to the fire pit at sunrise and spun around, like a dervish. I felt the glistening light splash off my skin and my jacket and whip out into the yard, splatter against the orange and yellow and chrome green autumn leaves. I could taste that rosy colour and it was sweet, sweet, sweet. Nectar.

Sol climbed into red-orange, coral and brilliant blue and, then, that light ran out from the sun and filtered down and away from the sun, filtering down and around the trees and their remaining canopies - spinning, spinning, spinning - until everything, everywhere seemed infused with rosiness.

It coated my eyes and I wept the rose color. It entered my nostrils and I smelled rosy brightness and I reached out and grabbed at it, rubbed it into my skin and felt each particle as it invaded to the very core of

Who I Am.

Namaste.

The fog seems to make the depth of colour more acute – light through the fog must magnify the colour, so our eyes travel <u>into</u> it, boring through microscopic layers of various stacked shades of hues, in order to see the ones our eyes actually do see. Maybe it's the water. Maybe the fine mist settles on a surface and reflects the light back, so it enters our eyes, intensified. But without help, most cameras just can't catch those subtleties. Still, I got some great pics this morning and for the past few.
SOME DAYS ARE JUST PERFECT/JOURNALLED

6-18-16 AFTER DECLAN AND DENVER: Forget. Maybe that's all our Spirits ever really want to do – just forget. Maybe, remembering is the thing our Spirits understand that we should never, ever attempt; maybe, we're wired to forget: keep the pain level down.

I know one thing, for sure, and one thing only: I'm meant to Love my way through this life. I've battled my way through way too many of those others. I need to Love. I intend to Love.

What happens if we don't keep our vow? Do we lose one another for all eternity?

All we are ever asked to do is Love – is this not true? Is this not thee Larger Truth?

In order to Love my way through this life, in order to Love YOU, I can't allow my ego to spoil my Love – but, then, none of us can. Can we?

Yet, right now, I'm remembering – "re-membering". I can't stop those memories. No amount of anything can stop them, because they are me and I am them. They rush me during sleep as well as when I'm awake.

From childhood, I had the ability to recognize energies from other times and places - energies from 'before'. Now, as I enter the 'end run', they seem to be crashing into me every time I turn around. Things have, somehow, accelerated. Souls (energies) that I know, I know – and, most of them know it, too. The universe conspired to throw Declan back and forth at me, but also to begin this current bombardment of Souls I'm now experiencing and all of it leaves me breathless...it's all about our breath, isn't it? Breathe.

It takes great courage to Love.

It's been three weeks since I left Denver, and you, Declan. Three weeks. Still, this 'wave' carries me all the way back to California and you, because I know darned good and well that you will not truly want to be anywhere else. I believed California would be where I would find you and, yeah, THERE YOU ARE. Mountains of courage – can we Love? DRAGGIN' MY FEET TOWARD MY TRUTH/RAW

6-26-2016/TRANSCRIPTION OF MEMORIES/ OCTOBER/1971/DRUNK/ANESTHESIA NEEDED/THESE PAINFUL PARTS INSIST UPON FINDING VOICE/NO/YES/THE STORY WON'T MAKE SENSE IF I DON'T TELL IT, TRULY

It hurts. Still. I swear to God, I will not cry another tear about this.

FUCK! I'm ballin' my eyes out.

I have to write this. Maybe, if I write it – put it on paper – tell my story – maybe, just maybe, I can let it go. Can any of us ever let go our past? I mean, our past is what helps define us, what makes us who we are, in our present. It shapes our energy, our ideas and beliefs: it teaches us, helps us choose our paths and, yes, those paths are many and they are varied.

Our past has a certain influence upon each of us; and although we can <u>use</u> our past to help us choose more wisely and to help us learn the Spirit lessons we asked to learn, before we arrived on earth, we really can't walk away from it, because it exists *for our purpose*.

Unless we completely lose our memory, each of our 'pasts' is a tool – if we are honest and if we choose to allow the past to assist us. It's always up to each of us. With the help of our past, we *become* in our present. Our past may not always **define** us, no not completely - yet, it does help to create our present. Were it not for this past of mine, I would be completely different, so, I might as well get it down and tell what I remember about it.

1971: Declan and I were getting ready to leave....to go where? Who knows - we're both Geminis and we needed to move, so we did. I opened the apartment door, ready to toss my purse into the MG and who's unlocking the door? 'Pam'. My roommate. She looks stressed and is very high strung on some substance, as she pushes me back into the

149

apartment. Wonder what's she's dropped this morning?
Gift from David?

Pam, says I, this is Declan Niall. She looks hard at him, and
I feel her anger and her dislike of him. Why?

Listen, says she, I gotta talk to you. Alone. She gives him
the evil eye. He feels her anger too, and walks outside. I'll
wait out here, says Dec. He climbs into the MG.

What the fuck is HE doin' here? says she.

I glance outside and spot 'David', looking at Dec and
smiling that weasel smile of his. How can Pam be so blind
as to 'date' this creep? He's much, much older than she and
we've been told he's a NARC and that our apartment is
being watched, because of him. We've known it for weeks.

Pam and I both work at a local pizza place and the owner
introduced us to David and later told us David asked for the
intro, because Pam is really great friends with Bill, a huge,
local pot dealer. David has Bill in his scope for a big drug
bust. Is Pam giving David info about Bill? I know she's
fucking David's brains out and, that alone, gives me not
only pause, but also the screaming creepy jeebies. How
could she do that? I no longer know this person.

I have kept these memories in my own Locked Box for
many years. I have refused to examine them, refused to
attempt to connect those dots, to speak of them, make any
sense of it, understand it for all these years. Not even Jack
knew this part of my story. And he knew most everything.
This part of this story had a huge impact upon the outcome
of my life – upon my life and, yet, I've been too afraid to
examine it, closely, for fear of what I'd find and just how
those dots actually do connect. There's that fear, again - ego

150

in overdrive. How did I succeed in abandoning my Spirit about this part of my life and for so long?

You know, it all returns to Love. Or the lack of it. As I look back, I genuinely see just how much I Loved Declan, even then, even at the beginning of our relationship, in this life. Did I, *even then*, have some intuition about how long we've traveled together?

Yes, I always felt it, that tug at my core, that Love. Always knew it – has this ability been a curse, as well as a gift? Yes, and amen.

I can digress as much as I want, but always, I must pick up that thread, because it simply has to be woven (told, revealed, looked at, etc., etc.). The tapestry will remain incomplete until I write all of it, regardless of how freaking painful it is.

Listen, says she…you know, we've been talking about going to DC for the summer and staying with 'Jane' (Pam's sister) so, right… we need to leave NOW…as in, right away…her look put the fear of God in me, because I knew something big was up and I knew she was not going to let me in on that secret…not all the way, anyhow…but it would impact the hell out of me, if I stayed. And, if I left. The situation had no positive choices, it seemed to me, in 1971. Even now, looking back, whatever I chose had embedded within that choice, some very difficult Spiritual lessons for all of us. Love. Forgiveness. Faith. Compassion. The long list goes on and on.

I can't go, says I. Declan and I have just connected, and I want to stay here and be with him. Pam, I love him.

Fuckin'a, you just met the dude. If you really love him, you'll go to DC with me, says she. She looks hard at me. When we pulled up, David saw him and told me they know all about Declan. He'll be busted if he hangs around here. Maybe you, too. You *know* they're watching our apartment.

I didn't just meet him, but I've known him, for, well, like, forever...I met him last year and, I'm not doing anything wrong, says I. How can they bust ME?

Your associations, Barb. Think.

Ahh, David keeps *you* safe, then, huh? says I. What's going on? says I...what did David tell you?

Doesn't matter, says she. If you really do love him, you'll come with me.

That's not good enough, Pam. I'm staying with him, right here in our apartment. I'm not going anywhere. I'll go to summer school and keep working.

Let me explain this to you, Barb, says she. We, as in you and I, need to get the hell out of Bloomington for the summer and if you leave Bloomington, then Declan will also probably leave Bloomington and he won't get caught up in what's going to go down after we leave. David says they already have Declan in their sights. He's on their list, but he doesn't have to get caught up in all of this – they want someone else.

Bill? Did you tell them about Billy T? says I. She looks away.

We don't have time for me to go into explaining all of this, Barb, says she. We gotta go and we gotta leave tomorrow morning. I don't give a shit about your 'boyfriend'. Call your mom and dad and tell them what we're doing and make it sound legit…make it sound good, so they say okay. You'll need to drive.

We can't take much, if we take the MG! says I. What do we do about the apartment – all our stuff? says I.

Your folks can come and clean it out, says she. Cancel the lease.

What the fuck? says I - how about your mom?!

You go talk to him, says Pam. Get him outta here. Take him back where you found him. You don't need to explain, just tell him we're going to DC, we've been planning this for a long time and we have to leave earlier than we expected because we got jobs waiting for us.

I start crying – you know those alligator tears that won't stop - the flood tears - the 'I can't talk or breathe' tears - the 'I'm chokin' myself' tears. You know the ones? I never, ever allowed Pam the upper hand in our friendship, for good reasons. Now it seemed I must, since I didn't know the entire story and couldn't take the chance Pam was lying: because I just loved Declan that much.

Pam shakes my shoulders, hard. Stop, says she. This bust has been planned for weeks.

Why didn't you clue me in on this shit? says I.

You love too deep, says she. I really couldn't trust you. Now look at you – I leave you alone for a couple days and suddenly, you're 'in love'.

This isn't sudden, Pam. I've been in Love with him for over a year – since I first felt him. I don't understand why you would rat out Bill, says I. He loves you and considers you a friend.

How do you know I did? says she. Maybe they just found out. Maybe they were watching back when he brought those bricks of Acapulco Gold here to our place and we helped him weigh it out and bag it.

Yeah, because YOU told him it was okay to do that, says I.

Right about then I began feeling very, very weird about Pam and my 'little voice' was screaming DO NOT TRUST THIS GIRL.
DO NOT GO ANYWHERE WITH THIS GIRL/DANGER, WILL ROBINSON/DANGER!!!

Did I hear that voice? Fuckin'a, I did. Did I listen to that voice? Did I Listen To That Voice?

I'm looking at this person, who has been a huge part of my life (until recently – until David) for three years. I can't see her any more. Pam has left the building and I'm looking around, lost.

I do 'pull myself together'. Grab my keys and walk to the car. Declan looks up: no smile, this time, like he KNOWS what I'm gonna say. He looks down. I get in and start the engine, put 'er in reverse and get the hell outta Dodge.

I'm silent.
The car is not. Screaming. Whining.

I don't know, can't recall, much of this next part. Guess it really was so painful, I couldn't keep it in there, you know, in my active memory.

I can't remember where I took Declan: what we said to one another. How it played out. I think I took him to a friend's house or to the bakery. I know I just told him the story Pam concocted about us going to DC - it WAS the truth, just not the WHOLE truth. "Lying by omission" -something I'd always despised and there I was, doing it with the One I Love More Than Any Other – but, I'd have done anything at that point, to keep him safe - and so I did.

He asked me, again, to go with him instead of with Pam. He already told me his plans to go to Morocco and he already asked me to accompany him. We don't want to be apart and yeah, I want to go but now, I'm thinking that really might not be a wise move on my part. I already got my ass in trouble once, the previous year, and I can't abide another brush with the law, because then, I'd have to kiss law school goodbye. At that time, I still planned on going to law school. I'm stuck between a rock and a hard place. Literally. In the weeds. Again.

Do I Love Declan enough to walk away from him? I'm not sure I'm quite THAT altruistic. I really wanted to go with him. Wanted to get the passport and make that journey with this Amazing Soul.

As it turned out, and as I see much later, everything really is fuckin' perfect, because what would I have done, if I had gone to Morocco with him? I would probably be dead or in a Moroccan prison and this book would be nada. There's that word, again.

And, yes, I wrote these recollections on a zillion pieces of scrap paper, because I couldn't sew them all together all at once, you know? Those damn threads, golden, or not. Couldn't thread that ole needle. Not that one last time. Until now.

THREADING MY WAY BACK HOME/TYING THOSE LOOSE ENDS/WRITTEN ON THE END PAGES OF "EMBROIDERY FOR BEGINNERS"

AUGUST/1971/SUFFERING IS ABOVE AND NOT BELOW/Antonio Porchia:
In the end, yes, I did Love him that much. When I dropped him wherever I dropped him, we said we would talk later. In 1971, we did NOT have computers/email or cell phones, so we actually had to plan and make an effort to communicate with one another. We decided on a time he'd call the DC apartment and continue this discussion. When I kissed him, my resolve to leave for DC crumbled and I knew, beyond a shadow of doubt, that this was the man I came to earth to find and I could not, EVER, let him go – then the voice said, "are you really THAT shallow, Barb?" I listened, that time. I knew what I had to do.

Many Souls await each of us, for many different reasons.

I drove back to the apartment and found Pam packing and screaming at me to 'get a move on'…we didn't have much time…call your folks…we need to go and get our paychecks…etc.

In that instance, I knew I'd made my decision. Pam called her sister and her mom and told them what we were doing - told her mom that my parents would clean out our apartment, even though I hadn't even asked them. But I did. I made that call and got everything arranged. They would drive to Bloomington sometime the following week and pack our stuff, since "we had to leave early to be in DC for those job interviews".

Finding all those bags of pot she stashed away was the hard part of getting ready to leave and I always wanted to ask my parents if they ever found any when they packed us up, but I never had the guts to go there: some warrior, huh? When she told Billy he could use our place and bag the AG, she had her reasons – she helped herself to about a dozen large bags of it...and, I didn't say a word.

I thought I'd puke.

But, I didn't: I partook.

Declan called and I cried my way through it. I gave him my parent's phone number and Jane's DC number, too ~ even though Pam told me not to do that. I didn't give a shit what she said, I couldn't lose this person; not now, not after all we went through to find one another.

We met one last time.

He was stunned. He couldn't speak at first. I see him, even now, with that look in his eyes. That sad, sad look, like "what's going on...I thought you Loved me...you said you did...I LOVE YOU, BARB...what are you doing? We waited for this. WHY are you doing this? Tell me...let me in" You know....THAT look. Yeah, the very look I gave him, decades later, in Denver. That eternal circle is, well – eternal, huh?

Hell, maybe you DON'T know, but hear this: he held me so close I thought we'd melded.

We locked eyes. He knew it was for real and he regrouped, quickly. Mercurial. Gemini. Me, too. I could not tell him the entire truth, because he'd try to get me to stay and leave with him. If I'd told him what was going on, for real, *he'd assure me everything was okay and he wasn't on any radar.* I'd never convince him otherwise – he was so sure of himself. I loved his confidence. I loved everything about him.

But I know his life is pretty much over if he gets busted. We're both just small-town farm kids, caught up in a difficult new world, neither one of us understood all that well; my intent was simply to keep both of us safe and, hopefully, we'd re-connect later, in autumn, when all the crap was over and we're both back home in Bloomington.

He told me he would call when his plans were firm and let me know where he was and what was going on: where he was going and when. Oh, my God, this was far, far worse than all those other deaths, combined. This was the pikes and the swords and the knives and the arrows and the bullets and lances and…and all the Warrior's weapons combined piercing my heart…but, sadly, not killing me. No. I was still alive. Still. And I had to walk this path.

And fuckin'a - what a bunch of crap. Now, it's 2016 and I'm still paying interest on that one. Will it ever end? There are no 'good' or 'bad' choices – there are simply choices, and we learn, or we do not learn, the Spiritual lessons we intend from those choices. What did I learn? If I could go back, would I do it differently? I could not – and, you'll soon understand why. This story is getting closer and closer "the destination" and I'm slipping I'm tumbling down a mountain of snow as sure as if I were on skis barrelling downhill.

Next morning, bright and early, we left out of Bloomington and began our long drive to DC. I don't think we stopped until we got there. I remember driving around and around that damned beltway and passing a huge water tower, which looked like a gigantic spider, many times – and, not knowing where to get off and get to our destination. It's funny, now, but sure as heck wasn't funny, back then. We wouldn't have had the money for a motel so I probably kept driving and driving, because every time Pam drove, the clutch lost considerable weight.

You got it – the clutch failed, anyway, in McKinney, VA…a mere couple months later.
IN JOURNAL NUMBER 32/YEAH, YOU *CAN* GO HOME AGAIN/JUST BE PREPARED

JUNE 2016 LETTER TO NT AFTER HE ASKED ABOUT DENVER/AM I ABLE/CAN I SHARE THIS PAIN?

Namaste Dear NT.... WOW
That's the longest email I've ever received from you – thank you.

Declan and I approached the meet with expectations – we didn't want to, didn't mean to, but we did. Anyone would, I'm certain. Neither of us slept the night before we met, so our energies were weird and wired to say the least. Forty-some years makes a huge difference on every level and I must admit I did not immediately recognize his energy.

I'd seen recent photos of Declan, so I recognized him, physically; but his cloaked energy left me reeling for a while. In all likelihood, it was the same for him with me. Even though I had no intention of masking my truest self, I probably did - simply to protect myself from - what? It was

159

an hour and a half later, when we shared supper and we were laughing about something; that's when I felt him, saw him, the genuine <u>him</u>, for the first time, since we re-connected in real life. I was so happy to finally <u>see</u> him. Be with him. His disguise was deep - to avoid hurt/pain? No one can jump into their own Locked Box, so... Maybe I'm over-thinking way too much.

He'd told me, weeks earlier, that I was the only woman who had ever 'Dear-Johned' him - and face to face at that. And several times. Could I possibly feel more miserable? No. I kept thinking about that, especially when he would look away from me when I asked a question. He'd said he put me in his Locked Box and he left me there...never took me out after the last time we saw one another. Am I truly out of that box, or did he just tell me I am? Not sure. Can he see me? All I really want to do is take him in my arms and beg his forgiveness. But, *why do I seek forgiveness??*

You'll understand more ie why I would walk away from that kind of Love, all those years ago, NT, when you read this book.

Anyhow, I saw how he was protecting himself and I just decided to go with the flow. I realize I can't push that ole river...maybe there are trust issues in all of this (for him) (for sure...) (for me – possibly...OK...YES).

So, that first evening we were both in rough shape and we decided to proceed carefully and with a bit more wisdom and caution than we had done when we were 20 and 21. We both agreed and he said neither of us needs to make a 'mistake' at this stage of our lives and, of course, you know I don't believe in mistakes (mis-takes??) we just make decisions and, hopefully, we learn some kind of spiritual lesson from them. No good, no bad...just choices.

After all these years of being the lead dog, I decided to drop back and just allow him to decide, because I could see the altitude was working hard on him, as it also was on me - I had a vertigo until Thursday - I was exhausted every afternoon and that is not at all like me.

Looking back on it I think he was wise and very kind: we'd both talked about 'how would we be able to leave one another?' and how hard it was going to be. It would be even harder if we'd jumped into this, with little thought as to the consequences. Certainly, I'm not ready, yet, to leave Florida and he knows that. He's, for sure, unwilling to leave California.

Do we have some kind of future together? Who knows? I know. No.

I'm ready to begin some kind of relationship, but maybe a really long distance one would just rip out my heart, so, I have to believe the universe knows best and will guide both of us to where we need to be, with or without one another. Maybe we can work this out? I've made something wonderful from much, much less on many occasions and I'll bet he has, too. We're SO much alike...amazes me, but no. If I have to force a feeling, then the feeling isn't genuine.

All I can say is that I had a wonderful time with him and I still Love him: in certain ways. I haven't looked too closely at it, because I don't want to set myself up and possibly fall even harder than I did that first time, all those years ago.

We did not talk about the past at all. That, primarily, freaked me out, because there are things I want/need to share with him but, it DID allow us to be in the NOW and enjoy our time together. It ended up being a time with no tears or feelings of guilt on either side. That's the stuff that hits later and I knew I'd have to face my reality or continue to suffer the consequences of lying to...myself. Again.

He took me to Red Rocks on my birthday and we watched *The Big Lebowski* movie, which I'd never seen. We laughed all night and snuggled under a blanket. NT, I still Love so many things about him, but I couldn't get a 'read' on him. The last hug we shared was warm. When I asked where it all leaves us, he said, "I wish I knew". I was never great at second-guessing these kinds of situations.

Why bother?
Does no good.

I wish there was more to tell. I wish we'd had a genuine and clear connection, but I'm too old to be playing games and I'm just not interested in manipulation. So much of who he was, was the person that kept me from him, in the first place. I wasn't interested in smoking pot all day or being involved in the 'cannabis industry' as old-time hippies try to maneuver their way to the top of heap.

I couldn't care less. If I've learned anything all these decades later, it's that I am grateful for a (somewhat) clear mind, which never relied on drugs to be able to live in this world – and grow, move forward. (Alcohol was my short-lived vice...)

This life – this wonderful life is beautiful, and treacherous enough to try navigate sober. I'm not so sure living it stoned all the time would be beneficial to my Soul. He seemed to believe he couldn't live, and live well, without some kind of substance. More's the pity. He didn't have to discuss it – I lived with an addict for over three decades. I saw him. It was enough for me to make my decision – an uncompromising one and the one I made forty-five years ago. Yes, the intentions I arrived on this earth with, held; they stood firm and I am Grateful.

And, I am Grateful I had the opportunity to see him again. I can close that nagging chapter, heal that oozing wound, glue my heart back together and move forward, with Love in my heart. I'll email you the book when I get a bit more of it done. I am happy to be going to the cabin: would I be happier if the cabin were in California? No.

I feel something coming at me. Again. Don't know how much more battered I can be.

You know I Love you that much, too. I've missed you; hearing from you, your voice...everything.

Meanwhile, know that I think of you daily (you're on my daily prayer list) and I Love you, deeply: some things never change, life to life.

WOW - guess I needed to tell someone about all this - thanks for being here for me, Dear NT.
Love & Brightest Blessings,
B

PS You know - I'm certain you must know that you probably saved my life this past winter.... yes, I was surrounded by loving friends in Boca Grande, but it was you who kept me sane and grounded, during the most difficult of times...I always knew I could count on you.

You may not believe in past life experiences, but I know you and I agreed to find one another and probably for this specific purpose - you knew I would need help and you love

163

me enough to be here for me even when it was tough, emotionally, and other ways.

I will always Love and honor you, through all our lives. I knew I could count on you, NT, from the moment we embraced it was crystal clear to me. Thank you. I Love you.

It requires great courage to Love, NT: Great Courage.

Love is the only Muse I know and this winter, you were that Love. WOW. That's *Some Kind of Love*, for sure. Thanks for the reminder, John…

Thank you.
B
ALL THE GODS AND PROPHETS TOLD US/WE WILL NOT BELIEVE/ALL YOU NEED IS LOVE

FLORIDA/2017/WHY CHOOSE LOVE?
"Your task is not to seek for love, but to seek and find all the barriers within yourself that you have built against it"
RUMI

That Love takes enormous courage is no joke. In Loving another, others, or everyone, we face possible rejection/hurt/pain/ego crap/rejection/hurt/pain/ego crap - you get the picture. But in NOT Loving, we face not receiving, well…*Love*…and there's a lotta stuff, great stuff, which accompanies Love: faith, and hope, and thoughtfulness, and kindness, and compassion, and forgiveness, and patience, and understanding, and tolerance…all the feel-good stuff.

I don't know about you, but I choose Love, every time.

LOVING MY WAY THROUGH THIS LIFE/LOVIN' MY WAY BACK TO YOU, BABE…SOUNDS LIKE A SONG, AGAIN

IRE/975AD/TAKING THE LONG WAY HOME:
Dermot. He must, truly, have but one goal in order to sustain his eternal existence and that is to take me down. How can a brother, a vowed advocate (what lie is that?) continually exist as such an under-handed and mean-spirited human? I do not know. He cannot hide his feelings for my Dear Wife, Niamh, and I hope he will do nothing rash. She and I have no secrets and I cannot even consider what I might do if he were to make threats or advances upon her, especially now, as we once again, start out for the killing fields of war.

WEEKS LATER: Why, this continual dream, these witchy hour terrors? Where is this place I am whisked to, so often? Who are these odd beings? Why do I feel helpless when I am the mightiest man alive, now, in Ire? U'Neill has no edge more than I, and yet, these creatures remove me from my bed, take me somewhere unfamiliar – I know not where – and I am bound, left alone and helpless. Alone with my own thoughts and demons.

What place is this? This is a place of FEAR. This is the place where fear was born. Only Beircheart could understand my trepidations: he has seen what dwells inside me. I would face all the warriors in Ireland, if I knew it would keep me far from this strange place. This place of the unknown. God, save me from this terror!

Last week, I watched U'Neill lead his clan across the River Nore – he has now entered our territory and come into our sacred Southern lands. Some of my men made a wide circle around them and cut them off as they proceeded

165

southward, engaged and killed many of them, but U'Neill managed to escape. Would that I had him in my clutches, now, I swear I would give no quarter and would, indeed, kill him outright for all the danger he has put in our way. WATCHING THE SILVER STREAK STOP DIRECTLY ABOVE US/WHO IS SCOTTY?

1966-67/HAIGHT-ASHBURY/SF.CA – Yeah, Jack was there - lived on the Haight, just a door or two down from the Dead. How could he NOT be there? He was a happenin' guy and usually smack dab in the center of the action.

I was a mere sophomore and junior in high school, when he was dropping mass quantities of fairly pure acid and drinking it, too – he said the Diggers used to serve it up, out of garbage cans, at People's Park (and down by the Bay?). He told me so much stuff about those hippie days and I just wish I'd recorded all of it, but, sadly, didn't.

Jack had the most amazing memory – photographic and on all fronts, all levels – that I've ever witnessed. He used to swear it was because of all that acid he consumed – maybe it was. That wasn't a good enough reason, for me.

My mind keeps revisiting the profound sense I've always had, about how in the world Jack and I ever met; I mean, it's always the same, isn't it? If one small incident hadn't happened, one of us not living one moment we lived; one of us not going that one place, which made all the difference in the world…just one thing different and we might never have crossed paths, met, saw one another in the first place.

I keep thinking what it was like, back decades ago: the waiting, the wondering, the exchange of letters, the waiting,

166

the wondering, the immense hassle of even attempting to find someone, of traveling somewhere distant. Makes my head spin.

But I know I did that stuff. So did you. Or, your mom.

If Jack had gone to California (why is that state so damn pivotal, for me?) and stayed, instead of going back and forth and finally deciding it was not the place for him. If I'd moved to California, back in the early 1980's, as I had considered doing? Questions. No answers. Except simply living.

If Jack had not decided to tackle his drug addictions; his alcohol addiction; his emotional issues; any number of things he (we) desperately needed to examine, in order to live this life with some sense of Spiritual clarity…wow, there wouldn't have been a Jack and Barbara. And that would have been so damn sad (for us) not to see what we had inside ourselves, aching to jump out and into reality. All that art, those artistic expressions, the poetry, paintings, sculptures, scripts, jewelry, prints, carvings – none of it borne.

I'm incredibly Grateful we shared the time we shared: incredibly Grateful.

I can't ever seem to explain it to my, or anyone's, satisfaction.

I don't believe in "one and onlys", I know there are many, many energies, many souls, I could've successfully lived those years with, but I found Jack and he found me and, together, we made something: wasn't the first time and it won't be the last.

167

I am the better child, the better mother, sibling, friend, gallerist, the better writer, poet, the better artist, the better everything, because Jack and I met, made and kept our promises (mostly) and developed the synergy between us, which was already there when we met and fell in Love...we had always been in Love.

We remembered and we honored the promise made, eons ago.

Jack

By

Barbara Helvey Hughes

(from notebook, April 1994)

I have felt the grace of your movement
The touch of your hand as it traces my spine.
I have shivered at your glance, and glare:
The power of your spirit, unleashed into the world.

I have welcomed the warm breath of your desire
Against the nape of my neck
I have wanted you, taken you, exalted you.
I have loved you.
I have witnessed your attempt to kill our love
Shouting tiny bullets, shot in blinded rage.
I have despised you, cried and mourned over you –
But I have always loved you.

I have accompanied you to places only kindred spirits find
And I have traveled back from eternity on the
Light of moonbeams.
I have wrapped you in my essence and left you for dead.
I have removed the shroud and found you alive again.
I have walked away many times over, in my mind
And returned to find you trying to find yourself.
Yet always, I have loved you.

The murmuring passion of my soul may not be
The passion, which speaks to yours:
Yet, we are bound in this life, as before, in others.
By what miracle, what angel's grace, do we attempt to
Find our path?

Tread gently upon my soul, for it is fragile
And I have become cautious as the years dwell and fade.
This love I have given – I have given only to you.
You are the light, beckoning my soul.
You are the very fabric of my being.
You are the unrelenting energy, which caught me off-guard
And won my heart,
And always, I have loved you.

The measure of our success is seldom the easy stuff – it's
the difficult steps – the one foot in front of the other kinda
stuff: especially when it would be easier and more
convenient and much less painful and take much less effort
- to walk away, to "cut and run" instead of staying the
course. That's the *courage of Love*, as I see it.

The larger lesson, then, might be the grace we gain, when
we have faith enough to let go of the ones we Love so very
deeply – and, move forward along our chosen paths,
knowing they have completed this, their journey. We bring
forth the courage, the faith to carry on, to Love again, to
finish walking our road, whether alone or with another.
Yeah, the road <u>does</u> go ever on and on….and, on and
on…JRR knew, and he told us.

It's never our successes which define us – it's our losses and
how we choose to grow, to learn, to move forward, or not,
because of them. Or, perhaps, *in spite* of them/ *to spite* them:

spite can be a powerful motivator, for some. There's that ego vs. Love, again.

Some relationships end in abandonment, divorce, and any number of possible endings. I'm certain I lived many existences, where mine did not last, were not seen to their conclusions, not honoured, where I let people down, trampled them, hurt them, killed parts of their Souls; but I also lifted, treasured and cherished many of them. It's all alright.

Sometimes we 'move on', sometimes we 'move forward'. Moving forward involves learning the lesson we asked to learn and it's always good to remember that we don't get to choose HOW we learn those lessons we requested: aye, there's that damn rub!
SOMETIMES LOVE SAYS I'M SORRY/SOMETIMES LOVE JUST KEEPS SILENT

6-27-2016 THE HARDEST PART IS WAITING TO BE TOLD:
I never looked at this and only shared a part of it with Declan, because it had to do with him, but now it begs to be told, in its entirety.

This is the painful stuff I've carried and still I carry, and it weighs me down, down, down. When, recently, I confessed it all to my brother, he says, I can't believe you kept this to yourself all these years, Barb…and, you, the writer and talker…the communicator.

Well, says I, I did tell Sis and one or two girlfriends over the years, but not ALL of it. Yeah, I held it. I carried it – carried that weight. A long time. Secrets: how heavy they weigh on us. This is the right time to share mine.

Maybe this book will help someone. All I can hope.

Okay, so, it's time to look this terrible truth right in the eye:

Pam and I first got jobs as part of a HoJo housekeeping staff – we were maids and cleaned rooms. Nasty. I couldn't let that last long and, soon, had a job selling *Encyclopedia Britannica* at Walter Reed Hospital – what I witnessed, there, while our nation was in the throes of Viet Nam, continues to haunt my dreams.

I grew up reading EB. On rainy days, I'd pull out a random volume and read away, so I was a natural for that job. I did fairly well for them, but not so well for me, and my psyche. That was summer, 1971 and our troops, our boys (there were no women in combat, back then) were returning home, wounded, in droves. Just boys – young boys; doves arriving in sickeningly wounded droves.

When I say wounded, I mean most of them were either missing a limb or multiple limbs, or returned with shrapnel wounds so grievous and intense it was all I could do not to burst into tears when I'd meet one or go visit one of them. I loved those guys – I loved their courage, their love of country, their positive attitude. I always wondered, when reality set in after they left the hospital and left all their safety nets, how did these brave, gullible young men fare?

It was a difficult summer on all fronts. After we'd been staying at Jane's for a while, I was told I had to leave – the apartment just wasn't big enough for all of us and that was the truth. I can't even recall where I slept.

Of course, I was incredibly blindsided. I'd just found out, from Pam, that Billy T had been arrested. Devastation. I could never look at her, again – to this day I have not

171

spoken with her. I did, however, receive several letters from Bill and kept up with him for a while.

I'd become friends with the woman who had four children and lived above us – sort of 'friends' that is: she could scare the hell outta me, with just a look. She wore a huge Afro and John Lennon blue lens sunglasses and could wither anyone with her evil eye. She was from the Caribbean and was married to a US serviceman.

I got to know her pretty well. After Declan visited and then left for Morocco and my parents and sister visited and I was asked to leave the apartment, well, she stepped in and saved me by giving me her friendship and a bed in her apartment. Where, every morning in late July, I began my day by throwing up, violently. Wonder what bug I picked up from the kids? thought I.

One morning my hostess, Gabriella, stood in the doorway as I wretched, shaking her head and asked, When was the last time you had sex, Barb? I startle. You're pregnant, says she.

My heart raced as I argued, I can't be. Declan was my first. You don't get pregnant the first time…uh, do you? Only Declan, Gabriella, only Dec…

Gabriella had a deep, mellow laugh, which sent a shiver up my spine, because it seemed to be born in the ground below her. She laughed that laugh. I shivered and, in an instance, I realized Gabe was right – suddenly, I had no doubt: I was pregnant with Declan's child! I was ecstatic! Amazing! Wonderful! Expecting Declan's child! Oh…shit! I saw my young life flash before my eyes. Where is Declan?

172

OMG – Oh, no - he's nowhere around and how in the world can I possibly find him? He could be anywhere and I haven't a clue as to how to reach him and I have to talk with him, share this with him and ask his advice about what to do. Should I go back to Indiana and wait for him? Should I call his mom and hope he calls her so she can tell him to call me? OMG! What should I do?

I am alone and pregnant and the man I love is in a country that dwells in the Middle Ages – Morocco. Declan has to know, before I do anything.

OMG – how can I possibly tell my parents? They just left from visiting me and I was sick every morning, then, too. I didn't have a clue. SO naïve. I figured I'd better call Declan's Mom and wait and see if she can reach him. If he can reach me. Those were my thought processes as a twenty-year old…heck, I hadn't even seen a doctor and didn't truly know if I really was pregnant; but I knew. I never had one doubt about it and even though it might seem to an outsider that this was a truly negative thing, for me, it was wonderful! Briefly. Then the tearful tsunami arrived and…

All I could do was cry. I still had to work, so Gabriella found me a free clinic and I got an appointment. She also went with me to the doctor's visit and was with me after I got the news: Yes, I was pregnant; but there was some really bad news, too, and that was that I had also contracted an extremely virulent strain of VD and the fetus was nearly destroyed, already. That was the very first time I actually felt my heart break inside my chest. The doctor informed me I would need to have a "D&C" in DC and have it as soon as possible, to avoid further medical complications.

I really could not tell my mom - a devout and strict Catholic. I was genuinely in Love and ALONE.

Life is all about breath and I could not breathe.

Gabriella held me so I wouldn't fall, wouldn't faint. I was blinded by the darkness, which had just started to make its way toward me; just started drawing down the curtain, blocking all that beautiful and necessary Light, you know, the Light we're known for, when we're young and vibrant and full of Love, hope and wonder. That Light was quickly retreating and that dark was just doing what this stuff does – filling the void. I could not breathe and bent full over, clutched my guts, wailed and started screaming his name: DECLAN! DECLAN! DECLAN!
I think I dropped to my knees. It's a blur.

I looked up at the doc and I swear he'd positioned his hand as if he was going to slap me silly. I recoiled, calmed and gathered myself as much as possible and he looked me hard in the eyes and he says: This is what we're going to do – I have you scheduled for a D&C in four days. You will, until then, receive very heavy, daily, doses of penicillin.

Is that an abortion? says I.

Yes, he replies. You're eight weeks in, so we have time.

Eight weeks – yep, my birthday was exactly eight weeks ago. Some things are easy. Some aren't. The rest of this would not be easy, by any stretch of anyone's imagination.

Through gut-wrenching tears, I said, I don't have the money for an abortion. My parents can't know about this and I have to find my boyfriend and talk with him! This is his

174

baby, too! Yep, there I was, standing on the corner of Broken and Heart.

Do you want to die? says the doc. He leaned in real close to me. His breath pelted me.

Of course not! says I.

I believe this strain of venereal disease has done so much damage, and so quickly, I fear you might never be able to have children. If we don't treat you, as soon as possible, you are assured of no future children, says Doc. I later learned that venereal disease was at epidemic highs, at I.U.. But I always wondered if Doc was lying to me.

I couldn't reach Declan. I called his mother and begged her to try to find him and have him contact me as soon as possible – I did not tell her about the pregnancy, as I recall.

Mercy, I was so physically and emotionally ill I don't know by what grace I made it through those few days until I entered the clinic and went under. Well, yeah: I do know. Angels. All around me. The sweet nurse held my hand going into the procedure and says, Don't worry, Miss. You have plenty of time to have more babies. Little did she know.

When I awoke and that nurse was still there, I asked her if she knew if it was a boy or a girl and she says, Honey, it was a little boy. I'm just so sorry. There'll be more babies, Sweetie. Don't you worry, Honey. You'll be fine. All the time in the world, she patted my hand to comfort me.

I've never asked Declan if I was the first time he got a girl pregnant, but always I have wondered: was this his first boy? His first child?

When I returned to the clinic for the follow up appointment the doctor asked what I was going to do, now, and I was so naïve I didn't even realize he meant birth control. I told him I was driving home and going back to college. I went on the pill: at his insistence.

I never told my parents. Never spoke of it to mom, who was my dearest friend all of my life. But much later, way after when I got home, she told me that on a certain day (the day I had the abortion) a boy named Declan called our house and asked to speak to me – it was urgent. Mom told him I was driving home and would be home in a couple days and she would let me know.

Two days after the D&C, I was on the way back to Indiana. I could barely drive because the pain, on all levels, was so incredibly unbelievable and unbearable. (Remember…the MG's clutch failed on that trip, so I was waylaid and late.)

Mom asked Declan what this was about and could she help him. He said no, but he asked was I alright? He had a feeling something was wrong and he needed to know if I was okay. Of course, I told him you were fine, and on your way home, Barbie, says Mom. There was absolutely nothing wrong and you'd soon be home. He shouldn't worry, she told him.

Yeah, he intuitively knew something was up – I was in Trouble and needed him, but it was over by the time he got the message to call me. I had to decide without him and, really, there was no decision - no choice involved. It was what it was, and nothing could change it.
Thirty fuckin' miles...

I've never blamed him or felt he did me wrong – he didn't know, didn't have a clue, because I did not communicate

176

what had happened, accurately, and because he was in no condition to hear it, anyway: neither of us fared really well in those months and years which followed.

We, each, had our issues with substances as we kept being propelled back into one another by a ruthless, heartless and unfeeling universe. That's what I *used* to think, but things have a way of entering a truer perspective, with time.

Now, all I see is perfection – the absolute perfection in each moment, however painful that moment might have been.

However painful it was; because fuckin'a…those were <u>all</u> painful moments – every breath; I feel them, to this very day. I've wept my way through this story…

Requiem
By
Barbara Helvey Hughes, 2004

I have drowned in tears this time
Drowned and drowned in tears this time
Joy and sorrow, love and pain
Drowned in tears again, again.

I've been caught up short this time
No time, hard time, fleeting time.
Yearning, burning straight ahead
Comets overhead flash red
Drowning me in tears this time.
Found and bound by tears this time.

I have drowned in tears this time
Waves and graves and tears this time
Searing, salty tears sublime
Tears through years and years this time.

177

Pytor Ilyich wrote it best
Stirring, stirring in my breast:
Captured rapture slips on by
Heart wells up but cannot cry.
I have drowned in tears this time
Deluged and drowned by tears.

Those years made a huge impact upon me and, I believe, changed the very course of my life: my journey and, my spiritual development. It was the first time, of many times, I felt genuinely lost – rudderless, without an anchor, without direction and purpose. I learned that to be 'lost' isn't all bad…it's how we learn the important stuff - how we 'become'. Those who never experience feeling lost, generally, will never experience the feeling of being found – of finding their compass and, consequently, their way through this life.

How can we possibly develop Faith, if there is no need, no desire to be found or find our way?

Had I been wiser (?), or more mature (?), I might have immediately returned to Declan - joined him, but I didn't yet know he'd called our house and asked about me; months passed before Mom remembered to tell me that, so I just figured he didn't care. I began drinking, heavily.

We think we know.

We seldom *truly* know…
2025/FINAL EDIT AFTER LACEY'S READ/NOTES AND NOTES AND EDITS GALORE

2011/FLORIDA – We watch our new grandson as much as we are able. He's about seven months old, we Love him dearly and we're aware of some of the inexplicable things he

178

does, like when he stops whatever he's been engaged in, shifts his eyes up toward one of the corners of whatever room we're in, slacks his mouth, cocks his head as if he's listening to someone/thing, and his eyes glaze over - he just stares and stares – he's mesmerized by something/someone and even if we snap our fingers or speak to him, his gaze does not waver, he will not shift his eyes or look away.

Jack and I have begun speculating about what he sees, what he hears, what he watches…we've concluded it must be angels. He's young and can, in all probability, still recognize them, still see them, maybe even still hear them. How wonderful, for him.

He was one of my major inspirations of my poem, *Reversal.*

We no longer attempt to shift away his focus – we want him to savour each experience, because it will end too quickly and he will completely forget all of it, more than likely. I hope not. I hope he remembers: I hope he talks about it, screams his knowing from the highest rooftop and doesn't ever stop talking about what he knows and remembers. I pray that will be his gift…the gift to him and his gift to all of us. But unfortunately, it isn't likely.

What about all my other lives? A few, I remember vividly. A lot of scraps, loose threads in my tapestry. Or, a patchwork quilt? I don't know, but, the event, below, is how it all started, for me.
1968/RECURRING DREAM FROM
CHILDHOOD/THE REALITY OF BEING REAL

1957-58/LOGANSPORT, IN/EASTER SUNDAY
We'd returned from early mass. April, I think. Whatever the month or day, spring had sprung, and the air was thick with the smells of burgeoning life. I ran inside, changed my

clothes and dashed back out of the house, slamming the screen door behind me, as Mom hollers, "Don't slam the screen door". I know you know exactly what I mean.

Our yard was filled with trees and plants. We'd moved into town from the farm after my older brother, Ron, got polio. He attended school using an intercom system designed and installed by the phone company. Ron had suffered a devastating case of polio, which left him handicapped, and for all his life. He was an amazing soul. Many of the most important pieces of spiritual information I've received in this life, came directly from Ron (Bubba): like the intros to Gandhi, John Lilly and his Human Dolphin Foundation, Rachael Carson, whatever cool and interesting info I'd get if I read our encyclopedias. He suggested I should study Latin, because it helps with many words: a lot of my approach to learning was suggested by my brother.

That Easter morning, I blasted outside and the big maple in the front yard called my name. It had a perfectly positioned fork, low enough for my young body to grab hold and climb – and I did. Always wanting to see more, I headed for the topmost branches: or, at least, the ones higher than the ones I'd conquered the previous year.

Up, up, up I scampered, until I heard a distinct creak and then I froze. I'd already shimmied out a tad farther than advisable...always did push boundaries and this was no exception. The scooting backward only defined the creak, more loudly, and my throat constricted with the fear I might just...yeah...FALL!

I was about ten feet up – high enough to be thrilled to be so high, low enough (I hoped) not to do major damage or kill me if I fell. I knew it was inevitable so when the branch broke, I let go and spread my arms, mentally embracing the

180

freefall and physically hoping I would miraculously sprout wings and fly…it *was* Easter, after all and there *was* a precedent for people *rising* on that specific day. Unfortunately, I was not one of the risen – not then, nor now. I sank like a stone, into the sweet cushy grass below the tree…

…which wasn't all *that* cushy. But it was sweet smelling. Since that morning, I have always loved the fresh smell of spring grass. I landed on my back and it knocked the breath out of me. No one saw me. All the grownups were busy and most of the kids were never outside as early (or as late) as I was.

There I sprawled: disoriented, dazed, wondering if I could still move. I rolled to my tummy, happy to perform such an amazing feat after such a big plunge. My head rested on my right arm, but the fragrant grass beckoned and I buried my nose deep into it, with my face laid right on top of bright green grass. The loamy smell of earth took my breath away. Had this smell possibly been around all my brief life and I was just now sensing it? What else had I missed, I wondered?

In that moment I transported to another time and place. Abruptly, I realized I sat on the back of a huge horse: a very nervous horse, its hooves repeatedly striking earth, moving skittishly. I was only six or seven years old, in this current life, and my vocabulary was limited; but the sensation was genuine, real and powerful when I realized it was ME on that horse. Nauseous, I turned and gazed over my shoulder, back to a vast army of fierce looking warriors – my men. That was a fact.

I had no idea it was Ireland – I probably didn't even know someplace called Ireland existed. It was later, when I finally figured that out. My weapons weighed heavy on my back, on the stallion, and clanged so loudly against the shield I carried it seemed to reverberate through my body (under the maple tree) as the image continued.

Suddenly a series of still pictures, of what looked like real life, strobed through my mind and I witnessed terrible, horrific, nightmarish battle scenes – things I could not understand, or explain. It was many years, before I was able to write about the experience and, even more, before I could speak of it.

When the 'vision' ended, I was even more disoriented. Mom ran out of the house and I think she thought I was dead. She scooped me into her arms. My eyes opened and I cried as she carried me inside. I curled on the davenport, more than confused by what had just happened.

The visions/memories kept rolling through my mind, soon to be accompanied by others: in one I distinctly recalled that I lived a life in Africa, where I was captured and sold as a slave, but have no idea where I was sent. That's a recurring dream I've experienced since childhood: I'm caught and, in a cage, being transported. Carried by huge, strong warriors. Frightening.

These are memories which have traveled with me, since that day, that Easter morning when they first began to unravel: first began to show themselves.

Snatches of other times and unidentified places haunted my childhood and have continued throughout my life. So, when Scooter came into our bedroom and announced that this life was nicer than his last one – it cinched the deal, for me. I wanted more, yes. He would not give more, but in the distant echoes of my ancient memories, I already knew what he meant.

Up until that point, I did not genuinely believe any, or much, of it. I doubted all of it – every last shred. Scooter made me and Jack "Believers". We dropped Thomas and embraced Siddhartha. Opened our hearts and minds and Spirits and, you know, it's amazing just what we have access to when our hearts, minds and Spirits are open instead of closed.

I've told enough. The most important stuff, for this life, happened in this life. And those things must be my focus if I am to complete this journey I began seventy-four years ago…the rest is merely icing on the cake of life: this life.

We think we know.

We know only a miniscule amount.

All we can try to do is gather stars or stones…
2025/THE LESSONS/NOTES AND SCRIBBLES AND MESSAGES TO MYSELF

1971/BLOOMINTON/DC/BLUE RIDGE MOUNTAINS
…….I gathered stones, literally….and I have them, still, to this day. I keep them stacked on ledges and windowsills and makeshift altars in my studios and homes. Sis might still have some I gave her, too. Mine have accompanied me through all these years.

My stars shine down upon them now.

Life has a certain perfection we can only see by looking back: back and into our personal abyss.

If we are lucky – no, fortunate – no, Blessed, beyond belief – we share most of our most devastating, painful and wretched experiences with someone.

I was not Blessed to be with Declan during that most awful part of my life when, surely, I desperately *wanted* to be with him – but Gabriella appeared when I needed a Friend and she saw me through my rough, tough time.

Now I understand the notion that angels do, indeed, appear seemingly out of nowhere – and accompany us through those times which might just take us down for the count, had they NOT appeared.

Yes.

Bless you, Gabe.

Thank you, my Angel. My angels…all of you; you, hundreds and hundreds of beautiful Angels.

Writing this memoir has been like eating a freakin' elephant - one excruciating bite at a time. God, I'm full. Stuffed…

ONE LAST EXPERIENCE
Someone once said to me, "Barb, if you aren't living your intentions, the angels themselves will block your way."

I did not believe that statement, back then.

I do, now.

Several months after losing the vision in my right my eye, still angry and perplexed about my life, I stood on a quiet street corner in NYC, waiting for oncoming traffic to pass.

In a split second, a deep sadness flashed through me and I stepped off the curb and into traffic. I didn't even think about it. I just did it.

A forceful hand, or what felt like a hand, roughly grabbed my shoulder; pulled me back from the street and onto the sidewalk. Startled, I gaped around. No one there.

Frantic and distressed, I hailed a cab. It appeared out of nowhere. The driver seemed so familiar. He asked if I was okay. I began sobbing and blurted out what just happened. He was East Indian and a had a comforting look about him as his eyes riveted me in the rearview mirror, smiled a gentle smile and said, almost in a whisper, "It's not your time to go, Miss. You're needed here. Your angels couldn't have been clearer."

Eternity
By
Barbara Helvey Hughes, 2008

We've known each other
this lifetime hour –
who is to say where
our golden thread
begins or ends?

One minute, eternal
years reduce to a heartbeat:
time sparks from spirit
to spirit, knowing…

The lost find their way
through their gauntlet of lives.

These are true stories. Really. Those darned angels have been hounding me all my life; I just didn't recognize them. We get exactly what we need, when we need it – we simply don't understand most of our gifts at the time they are given…and, that's okay.

So, where does all this leave us? What's the ending of this story? There is no ending – I ain't dead, yet, and I am still weaving. Frantically, at times.

I've faced my demons and drove them back, in this life, with only Love as my weapon. I found Declan. I lost him. I found him again. I met with him. I still Love him. I still Love many, many souls. I am incredibly fortunate – yeah – amazingly, in fact. Maybe I'm amazed? I am.

I survived the Denver week and I resolved to just allow it to happen – no attempting to control, manipulate or influence any of it. I had a great time – stepped inside that circle and just flowed with life's natural force.

Sometimes a 'time' passes within our lives and we just won't allow ourselves to return to those past Dear Ones, in our present. Whatever happens will be perfect. That's all I know, but I do know that much, at least.

Denver might've just been my life's warm up, for this last movement. You know, the prelude, before the crescendos build one on top of the other - can't wait to experience that performance, but for now, I'm enjoying the tuning up part.

In everything, which I'm asked to live and to digest; and in all I'm asked to learn and all I hope to do – I pray I do all of it in the spirit of Love; because that, after all, is the point – why every single one of us is here, right now, in this place and time.

Meanwhile, other Souls enter and remind me that it truly is all about Love and Love truly is all we need. But then, I know that: still, the reminders uplift.

We grow our way into our Love.

The best is always right now, in the present moment - *always*. We just have to try and understand.
Reading this story, you should be certain of that.

Be an Angel.

Don't worry – you'll need your own, one day, and the Golden Thread you pick up and bind another's wounds with will, undoubtedly, be the one you will be bound with, too, by another.

Eternity is simply the space between God – and us.

The fuckin' perfection of this trip just fuckin' blows me away! How 'bout you? The F-word doesn't have the same impact it had, back in those far-out hippie days, you know?

Shine, Dear Ones, shine on!

LOVE.
PAX.
HAVE FUN.
Oh, yeah…there are no endings (how could there possibly be??) to any of this….
Only BEGINNINGS.

2017 ADDENDUM: For the Love of My Life: Peter.
See, we just have to wait.
Now I know: patience truly <u>is</u> a virtue. ♥

Release
For Declan

It's no good, trying to pry something from you, which you
just don't want to give, need to give, intend to give, fear
giving. Fear – the great immobilizer, eh? Then, why? Why
meet? Why did you insist upon this? Why are we here?

Outcomes hinge upon intent. What is yours? I know mine.
Mine is Love. Granted, not so very much when I was
young; no…I can't beg your forgiveness enough: still, you
know only <u>part</u> of our story.

So, shall we take Thomas Wolfe to heart? Believe
redemption does not exist? Look forward, only: toward
release? Walk away; never look back? Let go? Shine it on,
Baby. Shine it on?

If we could but believe in the eternal strand of Love's
DNA, the strand unwinding, forever; the mysteries we
cannot explain, will never explain, but which confront us -
as if angered, spoiled children when they kick and scream
because they did not, could not get their way, but, believe
they <u>can</u> if they just put up enough fuss…if we could but
believe like that; everything is possible. Love is possible.
And, not only Romantic love, for that is the simplest kind.
It is far too easy to become trapped within that web - no,
rather the kind of Love, which reaches in; grabs our hearts;
holds hard and fast and; then, *insists* we embrace the whole
of All. Everyone. Everything. Every place. Each atom.
Every cell - all those tight-packed strands of that twisted
DNA. Yes, the kind of Love about which mystics and

188

prophets and poets speak - Love of God-in-you and God in-me. Baby…that's some kinda Love.

This is where my thoughts have settled, because of you. You forced me to my core, the tap root of my Love: I entered a wasteland and almost turned away, almost left without even stepping one foot further. Something pulled me into it - a compulsion I could not release, could not turn from: I had to walk on, and move into the terrifying landscape of my Love, all of my Love. I discovered lost Love; forgotten Love; hurt Love; Love filled with pride; Love pushed away by ego; Love bound by painful iron chains; Love sunk in quicksand; wasted Love; Love humbled by those more decent than I; those kinder, more thoughtful than I. Those who easily forgave me; who Loved me, still, even after my negative actions, words, thoughts, deeds. Exalted Love. Passionate Love. Joyful. Unbounded. Spiritual. Redemptive. Love, Love, Love. I found the most radiant Loves were those compelled only by Love – no other motives.

As I walked (and, sometimes ran) across to where the seeds of my Love had grown or languished, I recognized the hills and valleys more clearly, the passing years became more discernable and I learned my Love was not static: it waxed and waned, sometimes it flourished, learned, grew and propelled itself toward everyone, everything. Sometimes it retreated. Eventually my Love world evolved, somehow brighter…more lovely, more tender, complete - and I began to understand. I see it, now: the path winds past alarming situations and experiences, but the sun shines intermittently. The moon graces all our ways so Light shines down upon us.

189

There you are. Here I am. Light and Love. They are the same. We are the same.

It matters not what we think we need, what we yearn for with all our hearts, what we believe we *deserve*: we deserve nada. Looking back forces release and allows us to walk forward: encourages freedom, growth. We learn to Love freely. Everyone and all things. *Thank you, for helping me understand this principle.*

It's the <u>only</u> genuine Secret and the sole thing we are commanded to do for our souls – and, for others.
Love, and Love more.

JUST DISCOVERED ESSAYS: Guess I've forever been writing about this stuff.

Rocks

Up early, I await Mother Earth's slight tilt, feel her spin on the balance pole we call an axis. Father Sun peeks over the Eastern Ridge – the Pisgah Forest. His eyes appreciatively glide ever so slowly across Mother's lush body, devouring her roundness, reflecting along her sacred circles until he spreads light over all her visible curves, mounds and swells, tumbling along the arc of her sides like a river joyfully discovering a newfound waterfall ~ bliss, at the falling.

I rise and stretch arms over my head, shift my body left and then right, encouraging my Spirit to shoot skyward, into the new day. I shake my long blonde hair, free the tangles woven on my pillow overnight and with lips turned up, I grab my notebook and pen and head for the kitchen.

Expressed slowly and patiently, the plunger extracts every bit of rich flavour from the fine grind. Eager, I pour a cup and head for the porch, where the first hint of light teases the Western Mountains awake. A moment later, I rush down the steps to the back yard, which directly overlooks East: magenta, yellow and purple waves paint a background for tall deciduous trees stretching to grab the first hint of sunlight along the dense ridgeline at the back of my cabin. Ahead of the tree line I spot the ancient game trail, still used by bucks and does as a sacred processional every autumn when smoke and loam lace together in a dance of fire and earth deep into the long, long nights of approaching winter.

Yes, I am a Celt.

What mist lingers, weaves into low crepe myrtle, rhododendron and wild blackberry bushes, continuing to hover and rest on the verdant leaves of the peach and cherry trees, now heavy with fruit, but quickly dissipates once light finds and chases it ~ evaporating it to nothingness, annihilating it before my eyes. Father Sun now firmly plants himself at the tall tops of the trees and I head back to the front porch and a nicer viewing height, to watch the West bathe in his light. It happens slowly. It happens quickly. It takes my breath away.

Mist's tendrils climb upward, out from shadows, pits and crevices, where they spent the damp night. Now, confronted by light, mist surrenders, rises and floats away to join banks of clouds ~ gangs of juvenile thunderheads bent on trouble, waiting over there in the North.

In the 'back yard' ~ really a wild and free meadow which surrounds the cabin ~ pink and lavender have morphed to yellow and blue, where they meld with one another, each sharing its richness and depth and gently spread along the visible sky. No clouds purl in the East and the sky reverberates an early morning clear, electric Carolina Blue.

I walk down the gravel lane to a small field I planted in winter rye last autumn. All I sought was an anchor for what I plan to be a wildflower or clover meadow, to encourage the bees. The Sacred Bees. Mind-wanderer, I glance back at our small cabin, remembering how Jack told me it is bolted to the solid mountain on which it sits. As the mountain goes, so goes the cabin.

My mind casts back, through the time warp of decades and arrives at me, aged seven or eight; I am trying to remember when it began, this obsession I have for rocks ~ a part of me, still befuddled I didn't end up a geologist, like my old friend Cody. Of course, with a name like Cody, you should end up a 'rock' something. But, my love of rocks probably started when I began sneaking off to the stone quarry, far, far away, down by the Wabash River (or was it the Eel?) bordered by the train tracks, where hobos jumped the rail and camped. I remember coming upon abandoned camps, littered with empty bean cans and the sticky remains of cloying peaches. I remember leading my motley crew there, where we used those remains for games of kick the can. Then, I noticed the rocks.

How beautiful they were, how individual, how they seemed to sing to me ~ each with its own singular note and melody. But some, with veritable symphonies. I remember picking them up, startled and excited to find seashells and tiny organisms embedded within them and, so, I packed them in my pockets, carried them home and lined them along my dresser top, inspecting them over and over as though they might reveal some distant Sacred Truth: they always did. They still do.

I remember the first 'big' fossil I found ~ I have it, still. It sits on the top shelf of a bookcase Jack made for me, under the windows in the front room of the cabin. I am looking at it, now, as I write. It's about 8-9 inches across and was almost a perfectly rounded rock, which was split right through its center, I think. It continues to amaze me and I find a delight each time I pick it up, cradle it in my cupped hands and rove my eyes over its surface. My heart flutterdances in my chest, because, you see, it is covered with imprints of beautiful seashells and when I was seven or eight years old, and stumbled upon this treasure, my brain could not fathom how a rock embedded with shells could possibly be found on the periphery of corn and wheat fields in the middle of rural Indiana. I asked my parents and they guided me to the Encyclopedia Britannica. I read about geology, paleontology and about what paleontologists do. I decided right then, I was gonna be one. Young dreams...

Throughout my life, wherever I have roamed, I have gathered and carried home, rocks. I try to find flat ones, which stack easily for my sacred, private altars. Does some ancient wise DNA thread remember Newgrange or some other Neolithic/Megalithic sites, where my Spirit wandered thousands of years ago? Are these dolmans, tombs and mounds I re-create in miniature so that I do not lose the tether of my pyramidal (or is it primordial?) past, when I danced and celebrated summer and winter solstices and the ritual of life's and death's sacred circle? Yes. I believe they are. I believe they are just that. The cycle recalled.

Of course, one such place for me would be Southern Ireland or anywhere the Irish and German Celts roamed. Scots, too. Magic and mystery embed deeply inside our bones via the avenues anchored and revealed by our DNA.

Here I am still standing next to stone walls I have the compulsion to build ~ this one adjacent to the field of rye in front of my art studio and co-created with my friend, Harris, last autumn. I simply could not leave without constructing it. My eyes run its length and I smile at our accomplishment – small, really, in the vast scope of things. I pull a coin out of my pocket and gaze thoughtfully at it ~ a triquetra: my personal venerated symbol for the Power of Three, my Sacred Number. Prime numbers ~ important. My mind wanders along the fault lines of thoughts aching to be borne.

Father Sun has risen and rides high in the east, revealing long, horizontal cloud whispers. A light breeze shivers past trees ~ angling for the back meadow, where memories reverb and echo beside that ancient primal Game Trail. There they are. Just there: The Old Ones. Our ancestors beckoning our hearts to open, speaking gently and with bright clarity: "walk softly upon your Mother, but...you come too." It's all about the Love.

A Sense of Place? PART I

We live multiple realities; so many in fact that it can seem mind-boggling, at times. From one moment to the next, we

194

grow, dwindle, change, become. As soon as we perceive the 'now' and vow to exist within it, it vanishes and becomes our past. Time is merely the rush of those waves of nows into our past, birthed within our future. Now does not exist. Except as a possibility: a thought, not a tangible. Time is a construct of the human mind ~ nothing more, nothing less.

Being mindful requires immense effort ~ super human effort ~ it is almost an impossibility. We live by rote much of our lives, as if in a dream. We develop patterns, habits, behavioural markers we simply cannot seem to shed: they more than just tether us to the constructs of our ego, they chain and bind us. They imprison us even when we begin to understand that change could free us ~ many of us are well addicted to abuse and negative behaviour. Some are addicted to emotional growth, some to hope, some to Love, some to anything egocentric. Some of us are givers; some, takers. Do we receive what we expect and what we ask for? I do not know. I think we can fly, but often choose to grovel. It's all relative. To each of us.

I believe we are purely Spirits existing for a time within an imperfectly perfect organic shell. Personally, I choose to be tactile this time, but I also choose to run and buffer all that gathered information through not only my physicality but also my Spirit, for deposit into my "Ancient Memory Bank" account, where hopefully, it will travel with my core on and on as I birth and rebirth on my way to wherever we end up (home?).

I've been travelling in and out of existences for a long, long while. Some, I remember with clarity, some vaguely (a glimmer) and some, not at all. I believe I've lived enough lives to begin to understand that we 'find' or connect with

195

the exact energies we ask for, to assist us in becoming whom we desire in this particular life. Everything is perfect even when ego whispers it is not.

If you and I connect on a deeper level than merely surface, it is because we agree and we both understand each possesses the possibility to assist the other in some manner. If we stay connected and a kind of Love grows, all the better ~ it is what we both desire and can use to help us fulfill intentions. If we do not, that is also perfect. Two energies must find common ground and align if they are to grow and realize intent ~ bring it to fruition. This sometimes translates to a life of searching and discovering. We all recognize it when it happens to us and, sometimes, we see it in others. Oddly, it can be obvious to us and, yet, not to those in the middle of it. For it to occur, it must be a mutual attraction ~ a singular force cannot force an intention growth.

The Old Ones, the Ancient Ones understood and this recognition defined their lives. What? That synchronicity exists all around us and all the 'time'. A dance begins ~ we participate or we walk away.

A Sense of Place, PART II
Kevin Fitzgerald's One-Man Exhibit

Something has been tugging my Golden Thread all my life. I have met more 'familiars' during this life than I can even recall ~ so many Loved Ones, so many re-connects, so many messages they have given me, secrets revealed to me, memories excited.

Here's what happened in mid-April. I hosted a one-man show for Kevin Fitzgerald. I've known Kevin a long while in this life and I genuinely Love him, but have no recollection of having shared a previous life with him. We met at my gallery on the Sunday before his Monday opening to hang the work. As he brought in his paintings we did not communicate, verbally. Every painting was hung and placed, in silent agreement between us, on the walls, thus creating a powerful exhibit. All the paintings were important and singularly beautiful, as I expected. I experienced a deep emotional connection with the entire body of work, but one painting gave me immediate, and then lingering, pause. When Kevin brought the painting titled "Beech Grove" into the gallery, my heart skipped a beat – I experienced a "heart stutter". And, then, it raced.

The painting is entirely green. The background, a dense and deep green, so dark and confining, it seems to present a depth of night, which must be known only to those who roamed and ritualized and celebrated night long and long ago. My eyes move forward into the painting's middle ground, where illusions of dancing shadows appear to whirl and gently spin from out of the shadows of barely recognizable tree trunks – suggestions really, nothing very overt. In the fore, a lone tree stands sentinel over the grove. This one tree presents an almost neon green partial canopy, spread wide, protecting everything within its energy range. The remainder of that tree's canopy, Kevin has painted in many, many shades and tones of green. This painting cannot be successfully photographed ~ it must be seen and absorbed. Druids celebrate among the shadows. I am not alone in having witnessed the ritual hidden inside this imagery. Powerful suggestions exist within the confines of this painting.

When Kevin propped "Beech Grove" against a wall, it was the first time we spoke, verbally, that morning as he unloaded the work. Our eyes met ~ he saw me shiver ~ "Where? says he. I beamed ~ "There?" says I. He beamed. "That's what I thought, too." says he. "I know." says I.

Later, we talked at length about the painting: a culmination of a series of similar pieces stretching back many years into Kevin's past and psyche ~ and, mine. He understood I recognized the place: I possess a fierce 'sense of place' this life and I'm grateful I've returned to many of those places which hold an impactful connection for me to past lives and grateful to feel their energy, again. Some, joyful; some, sorrowful. I have 'gone home', often, this time.

Here's my point ~ 'now' rushes at us like a hurricane of dervishes, spinning around us, assaulting us on every side, much of the 'time'. Maybe all 'being mindful' means is that we understand the necessity to stop, breathe, absorb those moments sometimes. That we allow our walls to freefall and come tumbling down, that we take a chance, make an effort, change, grow, embrace moments with passion and whatever faith we can muster ~ that we embrace intent and possibility. We walk with a degree of awareness into the moments of our lives. We invite clarity. We pause. Be.

Is it too much to ask ourselves as we tornado through our hours and days of this Gift of Life?
This question can only be answered by each of us.
This is a Soul Question.

It will reverberate in the quality of our lives ~ and, in the impact we may have as we walk, in awareness, as much as possible. Energy produces endless ripples.

Walk on, Bright Tribe, walk on.

Everything's Perfect: Part I, Chapter One

I cannot pull a rabbit out of a hat. I would not put a rabbit IN a hat, but then, I am not a magician and I have known magicians so I know how the trick works ~ there is no magic in it, it is just a trick, a lie, a slight of hand. Our lives are not some sly manipulation of tricks; no, they are full, filled to the brim with magic, mystery and wonder.

You are Sacred. Believe it. It is what I call a "Larger Truth". It is not a lie. There are no tricks, no falsity, here in this space I occupy when I write. There is only me and you and our thoughts and feelings: the sanctity of Love and caring, thoughtfulness and kindness, generosity of Spirit, forgiveness, patience, grace.

That evening in June, 2017, Peter said this to me: "There is no knowing forward, Barbara". Another Larger Truth. He was replying to a comment I'd made about wishing, at times, to have a crystal ball and be privy to my future. Of course, that's the ego part of me, the part steeped in fear, the part wanting control, the part thinking I know what's best and which does not trust whatever powers or energies or forces that be, to do what is 'best' and 'right' for me.

None of us possesses a crystal ball ~ we must put one foot in front of the other with only faith to buffer us. Should we encounter The Gauntlet, and we WILL encounter it at some

point during our lives, whatever degree of trust or faith we
have developed will, assuredly, come in handy. People
change, feelings change, circumstances and situations
change and it may seem, at times, that all about us is chaos,
where nothing and no one can genuinely be counted upon
~ a place where all of us exist as unreliable liars and creeps.
That is the lie. That is the burden of ego attempting to
undermine reality ~ a reality, where, moving into our lives
with faith and trust in our perfection and the perfection OF
our lives, remains the genuine Truth. When we give others
the benefit of the doubt, it sends this message: I believe in
you. I believe in YOU. Huge. It's the best we can do,
while waiting for the best in ourselves, and others.

Expectations are normal for humans. Maybe if we were all-
knowing deities, we could release our expectations. For
sure, we would be far happier and own a higher quality of
mental health without them. They jam us up, emotionally;
they play to our (ego) fears; they hold us hostage; they exist
as a kind of "emotional terrorism" we learn to utilize when
we cannot get our way ~ when we are threatened with some
loss or when we simply desire to keep those (we say) we
Love, in check and 'play' them and their emotions. Every
single human learns how to manipulate using expectations
as a base to achieve our desires. For some reason, even
when our lives seem perfect to us, filled with magic, mystery
and wonder, we still must generate expectations of
ourselves but, mostly, others. It's almost like a game we just
need to play. We must. It eats at us when we don't. So,
how can we unlearn these destructive behaviours and trust
that everything we encounter is absolute perfection, without
our interference? I'm not certain we can, but we can make
big strides if we try.

Forming expectations is a behavioural pattern we learn as children. Our parents, family members, teachers, authority figures all program us to understand they expect certain behaviour from us ~ appropriate behaviour. Of course, those learned expectations fill many of us with trepidation, because those thoughts, those words and those actions don't sit well with us and don't come, naturally, to us ~ we are the square pegs they try to force into those round holes and we just don't fit. What to do? Guilt and shame seem to be the standard defenses against those of us who will not conform. Cannot conform. Those members of society who think outside the box and never, ever colour inside the lines ~ you know, the creative minds, who are "put up" with because we are 'artists' or 'professors' or 'wild outdoorsy types'. Because we dance to a tune they cannot hear ~ Thoreau, Emerson, Rumi, Gandhi, Mother Theresa, Martin Luther King, Mandela, Jung, Hesse and Schweitzer come to mind as well as a host of my other 'heroes'.

I've learned not to engage in behaviours which make me feel uncomfortable, because, for me, there is seldom growth in it ~ generally it's just ego tempting me into situations that require guilt or shame because I am not ready or prepared for them. It's me, wanting to please someone else when all I really need to do is understand the perfection of 'my' everything, right now. I can only walk the path I've chosen; I can only exist within my Golden Thread of successive moments ~ as also, you.

When we cut through ego's false expectations and align with our Spirit's understandings, our lives flow again, as they should and as they are designed to do ~ as if our river, again, flows through us and into the rest of everything, which is the interconnectedness of All. So, despite the fact

201

that there exists no crystal ball to forewarn us of the heartbreak, the bliss, the pain, the insights, the Soul suffering, the Soul revelations we all eventually must walk through and grow through and accept with whatever grace we can muster ~ when we arrive at that place we just might be able to see through the veil, or maybe even lift it a bit; so the magic, the mystery and the wonder which are our natural birthrights, become visible and we meet face to face with this, The Largest Larger Truth:
Everything's Fuckin' PERFECT!

Walk on, Bright Tribe.
Walk on.

"If you bring forth that which is within you, that which is within you will save you.
If you do not bring forth that which is within you, that which is within you will destroy you."
~ Thomas

Wrote and posted this on June 19, 2017. Edit on August 23, 2108 and re-post on Facebook

Everything's Fuckin' Perfect ~ Part I, Chapter II (B)

It always arrived with a strange, cool wind ~ no, not a breeze, but a distinct wind blowing clouds across the sky, shaking treetops, stirring the earth and bombarding my senses with overload ~ a dangerous combination, for me, this wanting, needing to move, to leave, to go somewhere, anywhere. The smell of petrichor: thanks, Brian. I can't explain it very well, this need, this urgency to move, to break free from…..what?

It's been unseasonably cool here on the mountaintop at my cabin. I've been here only a week and awaken, most days, at dawn with temperatures in the 60's, but this morning it was 55° and blustery. My kind of morning. *Thank You* begins on the radio: enter Jimmy Page, Robert Plant.

"If the sun refused to shine...." Tears spill down my cheeks as I gaze through wet film at the Western Ridges of the Blue Ridge Mountains. Memories ambush in a full-bore assault. I watch them rise and fall, like soldiers ordered out of the foxhole and immediately gunned down without taking so much as one step forward: Gallipoli all over again. Only with my warrior-like mems.

There they go: I was seven and didn't even know Ireland existed, but I was there, atop a stallion and I was armed for battle, I was a man; I was fifteen and standing on a hill overlooking the Wabash River and watching Native peoples watch white men build a settlement. Twenty-seven and dying of malaria while waiting to fly into Cote d'Ivoire's interior and watch a sea of elephants move as gracefully as a flock of birds across the open expanse below our Piper Cub. At twenty-nine I stood beneath the Atlas Mountains in the Sahara, where the sky exploded with stars overhead and my breath trapped in my throat, gasping. I think I was drowning. Sitting inside El Greco's studio in Toledo, Spain; walking the bowels of the ever-familiar Coliseum in Rome, still startled by the thick, loud noise around me; wandering down Negril's beach when the only structure there was Rick's. Canterbury. Ibadan. Bandol. Places of my past. Ghosts travelling with me for a time. What IS this restlessness I have sensed since childhood? On and on and on they march, those memories. I believed I had 'outgrown' these stirrings. That they were no more than youthful discontent. Now, I'm not so sure. I am attempting to contain these edgy waves of urgency I felt when I was much younger. Do we spend our entire lives simply awaiting our return home?

I'm climbing the outside stairs to my Tilghman Island studio, not far from the beach. The wind stirs ~ a chilly wind, sweeping toward me off the choppy water. I shiver. Turn and face Devil's Island, now almost completely consumed by the incoming tide. Silent. I watch. Something drives toward me. I startle. Almost drop my coffee mug. Shiver. It rushes past. Again. And, again. Throughout my life. Stirring. Stirring. Stirring. Something this way comes. Keeps me agitated. Fitful nights. Restless days. I realize now, the immense efforts my Spirit exerted all those years, just to keep me focused and centered and in one place. Will I break free? One day. But not today.

Do we ever, truly successfully discover the means to quiet our ancient longings? You know, the ones embedded within out genetic memory. Subdue our wanderlust. Stop breaking camp. Ignore the call of what makes us and traces us back to our savanna beginnings. Memories of flying as a bird; of tilting in this breeze as a tree; of the weight and firmness we felt as a rock with the sharp teeth of the wind scraping our backs, as we warm in the high-noon sun. I do not know.

I must believe I do not walk this strange and twisting road alone. I must believe there are fellow tribesmen out there, whose cores quake and rumble and yearn just like mine. We, yes you fellow travelers, we know all about the Light entering through wounds. Some, still weep and run, freshly marked.

Yes. I'll meet you there.

Don't go back to sleep or we will miss one another.
Tragedy.

Walk on, Bright Tribe.
Walk on.

Everything's Fuckin' Perfect, Part I, Chapter III

"The Road goes ever on and on..." (Tolkien) And, so, I
began to learn about the concept of impermanence, of
change. It probably came when my older brother was
stricken with a devastating case of polio. That's another
story, but it made an immense impact upon me and my life:
one moment he was there and we were running and playing,
the next he was gone. I did not know he was in an iron
lung. I was three years old. He was six. Suddenly, my best
friend, my protector, my co-conspirator (yeah, even at that
tender age) was gone. Poof! No one could successfully
explain it to me. I could not fathom it. Old Spirit; young
mind.

We believe we cannot live without someone or something:
the very thought of losing him or her or whatever we think
we cannot survive without (and be happy) drives a sick
feeling into the pit of our guts. Yes, I have been there.
And, survived. Just like you.

I remember, years ago, trying to wrap my brain around the
concept of eternity. The infinite. I had great difficulty ~ it
seems my finite mind cannot conceive the infinite and so,
too, the additional concept of permanence/impermanence

befuddles me almost to the point of distraction these days, because I have lived through so much and figure I should be one helluva lot smarter than I am: slow learner? Probably. These concepts exist, for me, more as imagery than as concrete realities. I have started thinking about them as Light. Eternity, the infinite, I envision as endless light, sprinkled with glitter. Yep, there it is. I figure I'll be safe when I shoot off through that, because hey, glitter never hurt anyone, right? How wrong we've been.

Permanence and impermanence are a different matter. Is it true that within the birth of every relationship or situation there also exists the germ of its death? I am beginning to think it is so. Sometimes when I form strong attachments, I also foresee the weaknesses which may, ultimately, lead to its death or undoing. These intuitions give me pause ~ long pause. Because with that information comes the choice ~ to proceed or to release the person before entanglements become hurtful, harmful or painful. Spiritually, or otherwise. It's always Spiritually, for me, more than anything. Just how much pain is too much pain? Individually, that is the simple, yet extremely complex, question we all eventually ask ourselves, in the quiet of our long night. Do the benefits outweigh the potential emotional or Spiritual suffering? If everything is, truly, "fuckin' perfect", then we surely must take a deep breath and move into these experiences with faith, and trust in the process to lead us to the place we mean to be; because without it, we may not get to where we mean to be.

Yeah, everything's fuckin' perfect, but the road, which goes ever on and on, can be fuckin' painful. So, we suck it up. There's more to come. I will say this: having been a warrior in past lives well prepared me for this one. But, killing Love

206

is much, much harder than killing, in general. The lingering effects of killing Love bleed all over the remainder of our lives and influence everything which follows. Killing Love is one of the singularly most difficult things any of us decides to do. It comes with an array of side effects and residual karmic difficulties ~ life and Love are never the same after we knowingly kill a pure and gentle Love. It is as though the Universe places a huge bounty upon those ingrates who do it and they, forever, pay and pay and pay.

Just because you have spent years with someone does not qualify that relationship as Love. Remember this. There are many forgeries out there. Many patterns, learned and shouldered. Genuine Love is kind, patient, thoughtful, understanding, forgiving ~ Love does not, in any authentic form or for any reason, do harm, say harm, think harm. If your supposed Love abuses, then it is not Love ~ it is merely ego's excuse to keep you trapped. You choose. Nothing lasts forever and into impermanence we all must walk. So, the dying of the Light of Love might well be our first and finest teacher about impermanence.

Walk on, Bright Tribe.

Walk on.

Nothing lasts forever says she. You must decide.
Is there a second chance says he.
Have the courage to stop hedging your bets says she.
Walk on.

Everything's Fuckin' Perfect, Part I, Chapter IV

We humans possess many gifts, which help us develop and survive; not the least of which is our intuition. Most of us have experienced moments when we inexplicably sense danger or an energy targeted at us or coming at us: enter shivers and the hair on our arms or the back of our necks standing at attention. These primal defense mechanisms developed to ensure our survival. I believe they have mutated into something far more complex and (Spiritually) useful. Something which defines us as "human" beings, not simply "beings". When we choose to ignore our gift of intuition, we do so at our own risk, because it comes with a specific kind of responsibility attached – a tool we can use to deepen and develop our unique Spirituality along our journey within this time/space.

Many of the things I thought about when I was a teenager and young adult have never been reconciled, Spiritually, intellectually or emotionally. They just sit there, waiting. Sometimes I hear a song and some feeling barrels back to me, shoots from the depths of my 'forgotten' past, upward like a geyser and spills all over my current thoughts. All because of a song, a poem, a quote, a look. We catch one another's eye all the time, but we refuse to see. Some lessons are just more painful than others. Some more lovely.

I don't know. I don't know much of anything anymore and having admitted that, I feel great comfort and relief. I no longer feel the need to police my thoughts. I am entirely open – to everything. Great freedom exists when we do not seek to confine our thoughts (intellectually, at least) – it's amazing where they roam and how creative we can become.

I've become a big believer in sitting quietly, outside if possible, and listening. Looking. Clarity. The world shimmers all around us – how often are we even partially aware of it? Sometimes the quality of our life isn't dependent upon how much we move, but how little.

Be quiet and the stress falls away, like water rushing down river, toward the awaiting ocean. It abandons us in veritable waves pulsing away, allowing calm, peace and serenity in its stead. Nature abhors a vacuum. Thankfully.

Here dwells another facet of intuition, because something always travels toward us. Bliss. I sense it. I feel it each morning when I rise and stretch skyward. It sweeps up and down my entire body in distinct surges. I wonder at it and it always delights me ~ it's often accompanied by a remembered prayer or poem or by a new thought itching to be jotted down on some renegade piece of paper. I've begun to understand that, with every heartbeat, this is simple gratitude: a refined sense of recognition of how blessed I am. How blessed my life is and how deeply grateful I am.

All things, all thoughts, all people come to us embedded with intent ~ theirs and ours. It is up to each of us to discern what that intent is, for us. Why, for instance, did I read Salinger's "Franny and Zoey"? I was fifteen or sixteen and had finished "Catcher", loved it and wanted more. So I bought "Franny and Zoey". I have come to understand that F&Z came to me for one, specific, purpose: that I would be directed to, and I would read about, an out-of-print book, "The Way of a Pilgrim", 1947, translated by R.M. French. And, I would find a copy. Thus, teaching me the concept of prayerful action and gratitude with every heartbeat. It is a book, which I read every other year, and have done, throughout my life. Just so I remember.

The warp and weft of each of our unique tapestries, weaves so beautifully because of these interconnections, which we might never understand if we don't activate the recognition of our gift of intuition. Even then, the recognition of interconnectedness might take years to see.

For instance: where would I be, without YOU?

Walk on, Bright Tribe.
Walk on.

I look up. There she is. I felt her long before I spotted her. I know that doe.

Everything's Fuckin' Perfect, Part I, Chapter V

Death does not become us, but it can help us Become. We all experience a vast array of endings as well as a wide range of beginnings ~ we must have one, to have the other. But, the death of a relationship ~ any kind of a relationship ~ is still a death and must be travelled through if we are to grow, change and evolve. Of course, many of us fear and fight change. Many do not care to grow, they are comfy right where they are and many decide (sometimes by not deciding) to dig in their heels and live lives of penance and 'quiet desperation', and then, one day, wonder why. It takes enormous courage to change and even more to Love.

When we cannot be thoroughly honest with ourselves, how can we hope to be honest with others? When we fear change and growth, we often throw down the gauntlet or build thick walls which cannot be breached ~ construct something to undermine the relationship we desire, but fear. It takes tenacity to Become ~ just ask the *Velveteen Rabbit.* Not all of us possess those qualities and some of us simply don't care: it cannot be forced upon us by another; it must arise from inside each of us.

For those who do care and who do want to nurture Love, please remember this: Love is kind and cannot be otherwise. Love is unique ~ we each grow Love and grow into Love based upon our life experiences ~ experiences which no other has had, or will ever have and so, our Love is unique. Love does not pity, for pity stunts and disallows growth: pity is hate-full. Love does not lie, for deceit and Love are opposite forces, one instigated by ego and fear and the other by Spirit and Love. Love is reliable and dependable – it does not waver nor wander: it simply IS.

I have had my fair share of emotional upheavals and challenges over the past couple of years. These have awakened a part of me, which asks me to grow and move forward. But, hey, everything's fuckin' perfect, so who am I to complain? I receive everything for which I have asked and much I just don't recall requesting, but I must have because it came my way, right? Slowly and patiently, I learn the lessons which will ensure my growth. Some are painful. Some, blissful. Some, tedious. It is very, very difficult to 'walk the talk'; much easier to mouth those words than to force ourselves to live them, huh? That's what I find, anyhow. We all falter at some point on our road ~ hopefully, we develop the courage to walk forward.

Luckily, as these 'deaths' arrive and as we proceed through the emotional side and back into the Light, the shadows

211

lessen and we begin, again, to trust and see more clearly ~
and, to wish those we Love to, also, walk toward their
fulfillment, as surely as we proceed to ours. Because, you
see, endings can mask as beginnings, so....

Walk on Bright Tribe. Walk on.

Is that Light in that field, ahead says he.
Yes, says she: I'll meet you there.

Everything's Fuckin' Perfect – Part I, Chapter VI

What do we have, if we don't have heart? For, without
heart we cannot feel, completely. 'Heart' demands our
vulnerability when ego encourages detachment. Heart asks
us to be patient when ego goads us to fearful thoughts,
words and actions. Heart embraces tenderness, knowing it
proves our strength, while ego whispers tenderness is only
for the weak. Heart inspires us to open our innermost
beings, so we include others; ego assures us we will get hurt
if we follow heart, best to stay within the prison (of our
own making). 'Heart', of course, represents Spirit (Love).

We have no clue what will transpire at the end of our lives,
but we can be confident that if we have not lived within
Love's circle, within Love's unbounded boundaries and
taken chances, attempting to change and grow and evolve ~
it might just be anticlimactic.

Having heart really means having courage, doesn't it? There
are infinite possibilities within each moment, each breath.
Atoms bounce, jostle and reverberate around and against
each other and the result is a kind of hum emanating from
everything surrounding us and all of that provides the

background music of life, unfolding. If we are very quiet and take just a moment, we can HEAR the heart of everything, including us. We've all heard our own hearts pounding in our chests, but to hear the hum of life around us is a magical and magnificent thing. Never doubt it ~ everything has heart. Everyone has heart: some just won't activate it and prefer living marginally. And that's okay. It's all perfect.

For me, one of the wonderful discoveries of my life was when I realized I could not only sense heart in another, not only hear it, but also FEEL it. There is a unique and different wave length associated with heart, just as with fear. I have felt fear, often, in others as well as in myself. And, I have felt heart (courage), too ~ it is a beautiful thing. A higher note.

It all returns to the base of Love, huh? All that 'good stuff' is really a simple and elegant circle, returning to its source ~ Love. Those fields and that passion Rumi and Rilke and all the others talked about and so often wrote about ~ it's all just Love. "Just" ~ HA!. I hope you think about that as you walk through this day and I hope you walk in Light and Love. Walk on, Bright Tribe. Walk on.

Do you know this poem? says he: Yes, says she.

"*Outwitted*
by Edwin Markham

He drew a circle that shut me out —
Heretic, rebel, a thing to flout.
But Love and I had the wit to win:
We drew a circle that took him in!

213

Everything's Fuckin' Perfect ~ Part 1, Chapter VI - A

I seldom hear genuine, unadulterated silence. The hum of life vibrates all around us, and especially here, at my cabin in the woods. This small structure anchors to the rock below it ~ rock which has existed millions of years: rock which has been pushed and stretched, heated, melted and reformed, thrust upward and pulled downward through millennium ~ I swear, there are times I hear, and feel, this rock sigh. Somehow, this place silently gave refuge to rogue wind-borne seeds seeking a home, and that seemingly endless cycle of life provides just about 8-10 inches of topsoil over much of the mountaintop. How would I know this? I'll get to that....

I've been thinking about Love and courage. Courage. All kinds. The courage it must entail to go somewhere foreign, somewhere possibly no other human has ever gone ~ somewhere we are entirely alone. A new landscape. A new mentalscape, emotionscape and Soulscape. Places where we are presented with entirely new and unique challenges. Life bursting forth, but different life, like nothing we have seen, or experienced, before: a "Jurassic Park", "Dune", "Brave New World", "Hobbit" kinda place. A 'Manchurian Candidate' kinda place: a 'Notebook', 'Love Actually', 'About Time' kinda place.

Somehow, I've ended up in isolated, desolate places several times during my travels. I've stood, alone, on that mountaintop, or looked out to a churning sea, or felt infinitesimally small, under an upside-down indigo bowl pierced with stars so bright it had to be a movie set and I just entered some kinda alternate reality. *The Truman Show* kinda place. But, no, these were real places I stumbled upon and had the great good fortune to stop, linger and look. Even if for only a moment.

These were freakin' 'break your heart' places: places so intense and wild and free that I wasn't sure I could recover from them. These were 'suck the breath right outta ya' places. At first, noiseless as in a vacuum: such quiet as will break your heart if you must dwell within them forever. Something, deep inside, tells you that. This HAD to be how my expedition hero, Captain Sir Richard Francis Burton felt many times during his life. But mine? On a much smaller and insignificant scale ~ important, only to me. Because within these places, something stirred me, some emotion with such depth that emotional earthquakes, emotional tsunamis ambushed me and awakened thoughts and primal memories so foreign, yet so familiar, that it has taken my entire life to come to, even marginal, terms with them. Courage. Yes, a form of courage was called upon and implemented by my Spirit. Keeps me travelling on, keeps me watching, learning, needing, wondering, wandering, growing, changing. Keeps me. Just keeps me.

Beat by beat I become aware of something, some low note, some low hum ~ a vibration, more than a melody. My mind casts back and back and back and I find my thoughts wandering within a strange landscape, but I am not 'me'. I am an Ancient One and I stand overlooking a spot which no human eyes have ever seen. I do not think any of this involves courage ~ it is simply my life.

I have experienced these imaginings, since childhood.

A faint memory bubbles to the surface of my thoughts as I prowl to this spot on four legs, and gaze out across the wide, unobstructed view. I am a mountain lion. I shift weight from one side to the other and feel my muscles ripple and relax for the first time in days. This barren rocky knob, heated lovingly by Father Sun, will be my bed: so, when I collapse, the warmth stored in these rocks vibrates up and into my tired body. I rest my head on my huge front paws. Sleep. Comes easy.

Courage ~ the courage to exist, to BE, to search: the kind of courage fueled by insistent thoughts that there exists something, just over that ridge. No matter what form we find ourselves within ~ it is all the same, this searching; these courageous and breathless moments. So many varieties of courage exist out there. Some, entail almost super-human efforts, some unfold quietly, some are primordial.

My life has been immensely blessed with courageous Souls ~ I am blood related to some; Soul related to others. I Love them all. They inspire me and by their very actions, their existence, their lives, they ask me to witness and forge ahead with my own unique dreams and life.

I have thought about Love a lot since Jack died. I have thought about pain (all kinds), about loss, about impermanence, and gratitude, patience, forgiveness and ~ courage. A spark of understanding flickers inside me. Sometimes, it requires great loss to begin to realize just how blessed we have been, and are. The film of time, which has for so long obscured our vision, begins to dissipate and the clarity of the moments we find ourselves walking within, sharpens. Wonder.

We were blind. Now, we see, however dimly.

Can you see that field? says he. I don't see it.
Yes, says she. Open your inside eyes. Close your outside
eyes.
Love is the language – been trying for years to speak it.

On and On for Peter from **Barbara, 2024**
Little did I know you were The One I'd been awaiting. It
took my entire life for me to be ready for you – yes, it was
worth the joy; and the suffering. I Love you and with every
part of who I am. And I know you Love me as well; and I
am Grateful. It's funny how I feel, sometimes – like words
aren't able to convey my feelings, because my feelings are so
intense, so vast, so complete. I am deeply Grateful I lived to
experience you: YOU. We coil as one strand. We weave the
tapestry of our lives, then the one, now, where we have
joined. How lucky can we get? Pretty darned lucky.

Home by Barbara Helvey Hughes, 2018

Stars burst overhead and
we don't even know it.
Vessels burst in our brains
and we sleep forever:
cataclysmic events.
And, we don't even know.

Given the opportunity to Love
I embrace it – try to never look back.
I Love you without reservation and
with few expectations (a leap, for me) –
that fire burns and smolders inside my Core.

While heartstrings twist and turn,
eventually, they calm.

The Way unfolds and we
begin our journeys home.

I am a Poet and
can be no one other
than a shuffler of words.

You accept my letters
and arrange them to a
beautiful melody…
so, my heart waits for you.

Home. Where we wanted to be all along.

Known By Barbara Helvey Hughes, 2017

This morning, I awoke thinking of you. I do not
know you ~ not in this life, not really. You seem
familiar and so, these past few months it has been
an easy road we have walked as we talk, share and
become known to one another. How much residual
energy do we carry from life to life? I do not know.
But, once in a while, someone enters my life,
whom I recognize. I have stopped ignoring it. These
meets are important and I have vowed to acknowledge
them. It is not the face or voice or anything visibly organic
I can point to and say, "Ah, yes, I remember you!" No,
it is far subtler, less pinpointable: a familiar energy.
People often smile, shake their heads ~ think I am some
sort of bimbo. I am not. These recognitions are genuine.
Known.

And, so, this morning when I awoke it was with
gratitude, because yesterday's nightmares lingered
as I fell off the edge of my supposed reality, last
eve, and I was skittish to enter back into deep sleep:
needed rest. Then, you appeared and guided me

through my maze of hopes and fears and all I
recalled, upon waking, was soft laughter and a
calm sense ~ trust. I felt emotionally safe as I
wandered back to here. We all find one another
at the most perfect moment, don't we? We arrive
from out there, amongst all those billions of souls
and we may not even understand we are searching.
And, yet, we find one another. Again, and again.
Less chance, in this technological age, than in ages,
past. Now, we are energy connected by energy.
Known.

Now, Reader, go LOVE your heart out and be Grateful.

www.ingramcontent.com/pod-product-compliance
Lightning Source LLC
Chambersburg PA
CBHW030826020726
47499CB00006B/2079